21st Century Adventures of Huckleberry Finn

TOM AND BECKY IN ST. PETERSBURG

Carson Cunningham

You might think me dead unless you read a book I wrote about thawing into the twenty-first century. If you read it, you know I escaped Dr. Knotts, landed in Rolling Dunes, and went for a football championship with the Musketeers: Johnny, Ned, and Tank. 'Twas the day after that championship, what with Dr. Knotts and the govment trying to pen me in, that I stepped into a Greyhound station in Chicago. The sun was about midway through its run and I was of a mind to catch a bus bound for St. Louis. Upon checking the board, I scribbled a short note on a route map, waited a bit, then stepped to the ticket counter.

"One-way to St. Louis please," says I, sliding the map to an attendant.

While she read my note, I pulled from my pocket a portion of the several hundreds of dollars in cash I'd made when I hawked that Notre Dame football ticket.

She sized me up a few moments; seemed unsure as to what to make of matters. I wore a tattered long-sleeved shirt under my Rolling Dunes football jersey, cut-off khaki pants, and cleats. My hair was awful full. On the map, I'd wrote that I's running to my auntie's from my pap, his forty rod and hick'ry stick.

"St. Louis?" asks she, quizzically.

I nodded.

She sized me further. I couldn't tell what she might do. At last, she printed a ticket and pulled out a form. "Give the form to the driver. It'll let you travel alone as a minor," says she.

"Thank you," says I.

"You take care, now," added she, with a slight smile. "And keep that one-of-a-kind style."

"Yes'm," says I, a-shrugging.

I stepped on the bus, picked a seat near the back, and was waiting for it to roll out when down the aisle comes a big-framed man in a fine suit, with a fedora on his head, goggles on his eyes, briefcase in-hand. I knew right away 'twas one of the henchman of Dr. Knotts's, that shady scientist I's avoiding. The henchman worked his way along till he got abreast of me, then sat directly across the aisle from me as if it were no big deal, just a fellow grabbing a seat.

I heard a loud hiss as the bus started us on our way. Dr. Knotts's man put down his newspaper and pulled out his cell phone. He sort of leaned toward the window seat and talked quietly so that I couldn't overhear what he said. Didn't matter, figured I. I knew their plan. Dr. Knotts and his gang aimed to meet me in St. Louis.

When the henchman wrapped his call, I expected him to mind his own. He did for a bit. But after he noticed me eyeing him, he smiled wry-like, leaned toward me, and said quietly, "Look, I assume you're on to me."

"Umm…well…" stammered I.

He continued, "I'm gonna level with you. First, there's no sense in running. Dr. Knotts will find you. He has gobs of money and is relentless. Relentless." He paused for a few moments. "On the flip side, he could make you a lot of money."

I stared at the henchman but didn't say anything.

"I mean, *a lot* of money," emphasized he, leaning in further. "As I'm sure you know, his oil ventures are quite lucrative. To him, though, it's about more than the money. What you and he could do together; well, simply put, it's a chance at the story of the century." He paused again and looked at me for effect, before continuing, "And it's a story that is in Dr. Knotts's wheelhouse. He was already deep into efforts to bring back the Wooly Mammoth and then, *voilà*, there you are, nearly thawed out of an iceberg after more than a century, offering him an incredible chance to apply to a human being the science he's been pursuing for years. He pumps you full of chemicals and slowly brings you back to life, out of a freeze, as only he and perhaps a handful of others on this earth could.

You and him, together, can make this the story of our times, and maybe provide a gateway to the great elixir." He paused again, then said, "So, just make this simple. Come in nice and easy when we get to St. Louis?"

I looked at the man, serious as could be, and said, "Sir, I think you got the wrong fellow. I don't know what in the 'ell you're talking about."

"Get outta here," scoffed he.

I stayed in character. "Seriously, sir, I know not of what you speak, none of it, from the iceberg on down to this Dr. Knotts fella."

"So be it," says the henchman, throwing his hands up. He sat upright and went back to his newspaper.

"Would you like some of my candy bar?" asks I, laying it on.

"No," says he, rolling his eyes.

'Twas a sort of a waiting game now, reckoned I. He'd give me time to think and, either way, they'd make their move in St. Louis. So from my backpack I pulled out a book written by that Louis L'Amour fella. He spun westerns. And, yes, I do like reading now. Miss Watson, have to admit, done me good in learning me spelling. To boot, when I read my mind tends to work on things in the background, if you know what I mean.

I kept a side eye on the henchman as I read and churned matters. The henchman seemed ruther relaxed; confident that they had me. After a while, he even appeared to doze a bit. By and by, I pulled out my map and went over a plan that'd been forming in my mind. Satisfied, I went back to reading.

Hours in, I spotted a sign for the city of Springfield, Illinois, our only stop before St. Louis. When we pulled into the main part of town, I quick-stepped to the bathroom at the back of the bus, bringing with me the Mother Lode—the nickname the Musketeers had given the backpack they'd borrowed me. At the bathroom door, I glanced back to the henchman. He seemed to be soft dozing.

I locked the door behind me, hung the backpack on a hook, and fished out of it my all-purpose knife. Standing on the toilet, I used the knife to loosen the ceiling vent. Removing it exposed a fan and one of them raised duct systems. I pulled myself up and wiggled into the little duct space, tight as can be. Up there I loosened the two bolts holding the fan in place. A knock sounded at the bathroom door.

"Wait a minute," answers I, sure that it was the henchman.

Dropping down, I set the fan on the floor. Another knock sounded. This one more of a pounding. Standing back on the toilet, I reached and pushed my backpack through the now clear opening, out onto the top of the bus. 'Twas a squeeze but next I pulled myself up and out atop the bus.

Being as we were in the heart of town, the bus was traveling slowly. As I crouched atop it, it slowed to a stop at a light. I slid the Mother Lode onto my back and looked ahead. The light turned green and the bus started through the intersection. When we passed underneath the traffic light, I jumped up and hung onto the beam from which it hung. Swinging myself onto the beam, I stood and tight-walked along it till I'd fully crossed the street, beneath me only sidewalk. A minivan slowed to watch me; saw two kids with their faces at the window, staring, mouths agape. A handful of people on the sidewalk below gawked.

I'd planned to climb down the traffic light trunk, then take off a-running for the nearby Abraham Lincoln Museum. But I saw that a large statue of Honest Abe hisself stood jest below me, greeting visitors to the museum grounds with a friendly wave. So I hopped to him, landed feet-first on Abraham Lincoln's shoulders. People was really a-staring at me now. I quick-clumb down ole Abe, hit the ground, and started a-running across a vast lawn and up some stairs, then around a paved walkway to the museum's main entrance.

Scurrying inside, I paid for admission and stepped through the turnstile. A cavernous lobby greeted me, hung on the back wall of which was large works of art depicting Lincoln. To my left was a wing of the museum devoted to Honest Abe's lawyering and presidency. History class learned me it at the Musketeers' school. To my right, was a wing devoted to Abe Lincoln's upbringing, which, as Musketeer Johhny MacShea liked to note, occurred mainly in Indiana.

Stepping through the entryway of this wing brought me to an exhibit that detailed Abe's earliest years. I passed another exhibit, then walked along a corridor, near the end of which sat a replica of the log cabin in which Abe Lincoln had taught himself to read by firelight. Through a window of this cabin was a replica of a young Lincoln lying in front of a hearth. The flames warn't real, but he looked awful cozy. I yawned and realized I hadn't slept for nearly two moons.

Studying this cabin more closely, I saw there was actual supplies inside, you know, to make it seem real, like pots and pans and such. Further, in a back corner, across from where Lincoln lay, I spotted a bunk bed. *Beats a straw tick*, thunk I. 'Twas dark in that back corner, hard to see, especially the top bunk. An idea hurtled in.

Jest past this replica of Lincoln's cabin, I stood with my back to the wall, waiting on a natural lull in the flow of people walking by. When one occurred, I quick-hopped a railing in front of the cabin and stepped across a strip of fake grass before sliding through the cabin door. Crouching low to the ground, I sort of floor-crawled over toward the corner bunk. Stashed the Mother Lode on the far side of the hearth, out of sight, stepped on a wooden rail of the bottom bunk, reached up, and swung up onto the top bunk. Lying down flat, I pulled a wool blanket full over me and played dead. Unless someone knew to strain, they couldn't see me if they tried, especially with the guardrail log running the length of the top bunk.

Might seem risky, but what else was a I to do? Warn't gonna turn myself in and let the govment have the run of me; didn't want to turn and run from Dr. Knott's hench-man all day. Instead, I turned in right there in Lincoln's bunk.

Slept deep. Found myself gliding down the Muddy with Jim, backed by a strong current and a warm sun, a-talking about our plans for the future. Dreamt of being on that glacier, too, only this time a beautiful princess, sailing on a ship full of jewels and desserts, rescued us. 'Twas while I dodged a Golden Dog tackler that I jerked my arm and kicked out my leg, awakening myself to a pitch black, mouse-quiet Lincoln museum.

I gap stretched and yawned and listened closely to the sound of nothing, before dropping to the bed below. At ground-level, I slid onto my belly and positioned myself in front of the hearth, alongside Lincoln, so it'd seem as if we was both reading by "firelight." Only with the museum closed there warn't no light. That is, till I pulled a match out my pocket and struck it to re-study the map of rail lines I'd picked up at the train station. Once my match burnt out, I turned to Lincoln, told him I appreci-ated him letting me stay but that I had to push on.

Over the mile it took to get from the museum to the rail line, darkness gave me cover. Upon reaching the line, I walked alongside it and soon spotted the exchange depot. Reckoned a freighter would slow a bit before passing through, especially since a slight curve led to it. Waiting for an opportunity, I slinked over to a patch of trees. Sure enough, within half-an-hour a freighter rumbled along. Once the lead cars passed, I stepped out to eye the line. An open door on a boxcar a-came into view. I ran alongside the track a bit, jest ahead of this slow-moving boxcar, let it come abreast of me, and then jumped into it. I sort of tumble-slid across the width of the car before sitting up against its side wall. Rolling along, I gazed through the rail car's half-open side door. Green trees bathed in the darkness of night passed my line of vision. It was oddly sort of mesmerizing. It kinda calmed me and I half-smiled, thinking, I'm going home.

CHAPTER TWO

By and by I grabbed for the backpack the Musketeers borrowed me. 'Twas during halftime of our championship football game that they told me of it. They'd brung it to the game and had Johnny's little brother sneak it onto my raft. They'd named it the Mother Lode because they'd packed it with my bearskin and supplies: Baby Ruths, a couple books, matches, my fishline and hooks, and one of them all-purpose knives. Oh, and a burner phone with a charger. I didn't know exactly what "burner" phone meant, but if Ned thought it'd be useful, I reckoned it would be. Going to all that trouble was mighty thoughtful of the Musketeers. That's how they was. And now, here I was a-pulling that bearskin out from it to wrap around my shoulders.

Soon, I caught myself dozing. By and by, I slept a mite.

I awoke of a sudden, worried that we'd rolled past St. Petersburg. Popping up and stepping over to the edge of the car, I leaned out to scan the terrain, the morning sun giving me a good view. From what I could tell, St. Petersburg was yet to come. Sure enough, after rolling along another half hour or so, I spotted, up ahead a stretch, the town coming into view, the Muddy too, awful wide and powerful. We crossed the river's massive breadth and slowed at a bend atop St. Petersburg.

Still at the box car's edge as we made the curve, I felt my heart a-thumping—this jump warn't as difficult as the one I'd made into the Detroit River, but it warn't nuthin, either. I wrapped the bearskin around my shoulders for protection, gently lobbed the Mother Lode out of the train, then jumped. For a few brief moments I's a-flying through the air again, free as a bird. I rolled through the brunt of meeting the dirt-packed ground, but it still thumped me pretty good. Thankfully, my bearskin kept me from getting scraped up. I found the Mother Lode and skirted into the forest's edge and into the deep woods. There I went searching for Pap's old cabin, more a shack really.

Took some work, but I found the cabin in a thick stretch of forest. It looked a bit rickety and had ivy growing all over its walls. Still, it stood—and only a few hundred yards from the Mighty, with St. Petersburg less than a mile below. A fine spot.

Having trudged through the overgrowth leading to the cabin, I forced open its door and laid my bearskin down on the floorboards. I saw that the inside of the door still had the markings on it from that time I whacked it repeatedly with an ax. And on the walls, faintly, was stains of the hog's blood I'd splattered them years back. The hole I'd sawed in one wall had been filled in with river clay. Pap's old horse-blanket, if you can believe it, hung across this old hole. All in all, the cabin hadn't hardly changed. And nobody'd been in it for many years, not for decades from what I could tell. It warn't likely for Dr. Knotts or the govment to find me here, judged I. It would do.

That first day at Pap's, I laid-low, on the look-out. Waited for darkness to nudge in before exploring the surrounding forest. It had grown in powerful thick around the cabin. I sort of meandered about looking for trails, reacquainting myself with the lay of the land. Far as it seemed, this stretch of forest warn't frequented by folks and was left to grow wild.

By and by I worked my way toward the river, sat by a tree near the bank. Through the light of the moon, I watched the Muddy and thought about the adventures I'd had on it with Jim and Tom all them years ago. Thought about my more recent adventures, too, back in Rolling Dunes with the Musketeers. Eventually my mind drifted to Dr. Knotts and his shady cabal of scientists out to find me, to prod and poke me like a live-action science experiment and turn me into a money-making exhibit.

Late night, I started a fire at a corner of the cabin above which was a small flue which poked through a hole in the roof. Resting on my bearskin I pulled out Louis L'Amour and, by firelight, read of a practical, drifting man, yearning to build a life. 'Twas like Louis was speaking directly to me.

Next evening, having slept late and lolled the day about, I slid over to Wal-Mart for supplies. I bought a pair of slip-on shoes, sort of like moccasins, a couple jerseys and cargo slacks, which I later cut at the bottom. Slacks is too smothery without shortening. Grabbed some soap with which to wash up and rinse my clothes. Picked up a li'l frying pot too. You can get all that at Walmart—and a bacon-scented pillow if you're looking for one. Place is a wonder. There was even a barber shop in it. I thought of coming back during regular hours, what with my hair so long and unruly, but I didn't risk it.

The next few days I spent exploring, keeping an eye out for who might come and go from the forest, and generally laying low. Saved my cabin fires for nighttime. One late, moonlit night I saw an old canoe floating down river. It tottered a bit, but it floated. I swum for it and pulled it to the shoreline, where I hid it under a snarl of thick brush, not far from Pap's. I mostly wanted it in the event I needed to glide out of town right-quick, you know, if the authorities or Dr. Knotts and his crew spotted me.

Another time, on an afternoon about a fortnight into my stay, I trekked through the forest till I could eye

Jackson Island, which set out in the middle of the Muddy, nearer to town. I'd been a-wondering if the island would make for a better hideout. But I noticed that steamboats regularly took folks on short rides up and down the river and slowed down for whatever reason as they passed the island. People out on deck would lean forward and crane their necks to get a good look and take pictures with their phones. I reckoned, with people gawking like that, I was more likely to get noticed there than at Pap's. Sure, in the forest by Pap's, there was an occasional trail. But, as I say, there warn't walkers about noway, not this time of year leastways. Probably picked up in the summer, guessed I. 'Twas plumb luck, I determined, to find Pap's ole cabin on what seemed like protected land, undisturbed.

To boot, near Pap's the fishing was good, both at the river and at a secluded pond further from town than the cabin. I would put lines out when darkness fell and in the deep night or early morn pull off a catfish here, a trout there. In time, I built a rock-lined pit for my cabin fires and constructed a little stand upon which to set my pot over the flames. When full, I'd read or jest lie outside the cabin and look at the sky, make shapes out of the stars.

One night, an awful big storm charged through. Thunder boomed so loud Pap's cabin shook. Lightning flung crooked shadows on the walls. Soon after, what seemed like a lake full of rain fell. I wrapped myself tight in my bearskin and waited on the storm to pass. Within an hour or so quiet come, that thick type of quiet that moves in after a good drenching. I lay there listening to that deep quiet, interrupted only on occasion by the hoot of an owl or the howl of a coyote, and realized that, while it'd taken time, my nerves had settled, my body felt rested.

Pangs of lonesomeness did grab hold of me on occasion. It helped to have L'Amour with me and another book the Musketeers'd borrowed me, *The Count of Monte Cristo.* As I say, much as I wouldn't've liked to admit it back then, I's ruther grateful now that Miss Watson and the Widow Douglas had learned me to read. Other things was changing with me, too. I could feel it in my body. I's growing up, stretching out.

As more weeks passed, though, my lonesomeness grew. Christmas came and went. The New Year rung in. I thought of the Musketeers and what fun they must've been having, and of the MacSheas. Oddly, the lonelier I got, the more I wanted to learn about what had happened to people who warn't around no more, to Tom Sawyer and Jim and the Widow Douglas and even to ornery Miss Watson. They was long gone, yet thinking of 'em made me less lonely. I thought of going by the old haunts. And I thought of finding new ones. In time, I settled on going into town.

CHAPTER THREE

On the Missoura side, cliffs overlook St. Petersburg, cliffs that give a sweeping view of the Mighty and of Illinois beyond. In town, below the cliffs, there are hills aplenty. A stretch of road is liable to slope upward here, flatten there, then go back up, steeper now, before dipping down again. As I walked along, it seemed like the general paths of the roads were in-line with the old trails Tom and me and the rest of the gang used to follow while sky-larking, running loot from marauders or robbing a band of thieves or some such Tom-imagined chicanery.

I kept an eye out for places of old, like Tom Sawyer's and Judge Thatcher's, Grant's drugstore and the tanyard. But warn't none of 'em where I remembered 'em having been. Taken down, reckoned I. In their place was bigger homes but many of 'em did seem in general disrepair. Several was boarded up, looked abandoned. Appeared as if times of struggle had hit St. Petersburg.

By and by I got on Hill Street and headed for the main part of town, alongside the river. Was jest a-strolling along, minding my own, when of a sudden I recognized a house. Only it warn't supposed to be this close to the town center. I stopped in my tracks for a double-take. 'Twas Becky Thatcher's old place, I's sure of it. I stepped to its front door. Sure enough, a sign on it read: Becky Thatcher's House. I peered through a window. They'd kept it a-looking like it did whence the time I came. Now if that ain't odd, thinks I, shuffling along.

The things I saw next stopped me dead in my tracks: I found Grant's old drugstore, only it too was in the wrong place, as was the tanyard. I even come upon Tom Sawyer's house, somehow placed here in the heart of town, along with the fence he'd talked them gullible boys into painting.

Finally, I come upon a sight that nearly brought me to the ground. A sign out front of it read: Huckleberry Finn Boyhood House. Felt like I'd seen a ghost. I glanced around nervously. Luckily, there were only a few people milling about, and they warn't paying me no mind. Pulling a deep breath, I reminded myself that no one knew my true identity—'cept for maybe Dr. Knotts and his crew—but they warn't around...well, at least as far as I could tell they warn't.

A couple walked into the little house, more like cabin. I stepped through the gate of a low-lying wood fence and across the small front yard. Reckoned I was only four years old since I'd last been inside. My pap lost the place not long after my mam passed. From what I'd heard, he'd barely held onto it while she was alive.

Stepping inside, I looked around. All the sudden, memory flooded me. I saw my mom setting in the corner, holding me. She was tired and worried. Tear trails run down her cheek. She held me close.

Turning my glance toward the fireplace, I saw Pap, carrying on, one hand waving in the air, sort of at random and wildly, the other holding a bottle of forty-rod. His hair was long, his beard unkempt. Something had angered him. Of course it was the liquor talking. His eyes blazed; his voice boomed.

I came out of my trance and stepped over to the cubby room in which I used to sleep. 'Twas smaller than I'd remembered. Next, I walked outside to the backyard and gazed toward where my friend Sam used to live, jest a little ways off from the cabin. Only his house warn't there because this old cabin warn't in this part of town then nuther. Instead, there was a large brick structure out back, off to the side. I walked across a patch of grass and worked my way down around to the front of this brick building. No whaling, 'twas a museum about the lives and times of Tom Sawyer and me.

People drifted in and out of the museum. The thought of going in myself made me ruther nervous, partly on account of seeing my old life put on display and partly 'cuz I worried somebody might find me out some way. I stepped in nohow and bought an admission ticket.

Spread out along the walls of a great hall near the front was sketches of Jim and I and Tom and other folks. There were framed letters penned by various of us hung on the wall, too, and placards explaining the times from when I come. Another section of the museum featured a reconstruction of the raft Jim and I made and floated down the Mississippi. Atop this raft was life-sized replicas of Jim and me and our supplies. 'Twas eerie reading up on us and seeing us; made my hair stand straight on my arm, sorta' how it does when you're walking through a graveyard and you hear ghosts use the wind to whistle.

Having strolled through most of the museum, I found myself in a hall along the wall of which hung renderings of our raft and of our camp on Jackson Island and of the Duke and the King and ole Miss Watson. I hadn't noticed anyone yet I felt a tap at my shoulder, and heard a man ask, "Are you a fan of Huckleberry Finn's?"

My heart skipped a beat. I turned and saw an older man with silver-blue eyes set behind goggles and hair which stood up kind of wild-like. He was tall and slender; wore a long thin sweater.

"Huck, umm, uh," bumbled I. "Huckleberry Finn…he seems all right."

The man looked at me for a moment. He smiled again, gently, and stuck out his hand. "I'm Orion Halley. I work, well I volunteer here at the museum from time to time."

"Name's Mark," says I. "Mark Finn."

"That's a good name," says he. His eyes twinkled a bit.

"So is Orion," says I.

"Thank you. My parents were eccentric. Scientists. They studied stars."

For a few moments we both turned to look at a couple of the sketches, one of Jim and I on our raft, another of our camp.

"Well, I figured you must like Huckleberry Finn," says Orion, "It's not too often I see someone as young as yourself come in here alone."

"I guess I'm jest a little different that way," says I, shrugging like it was nothing, like I warn't actually Huckleberry Finn.

"What do you think ever happened to Huckleberry Finn anyway?" asks I, gazing back at the drawings.

"One story says he ended up a justice of the peace out in a remote town in Montana," says Orion. "But I have never found evidence of that. And I've been to Montana to look for it. I don't think anyone knows for sure."

"How 'bout Jim?" asks I.

"Ended up a Deacon in the Northeast, and a butler to a well-known family which was quite fond of him, and he of them. He was a family man, devoted to his wife and children."

I nodded and moved in front of a rendering of Tom Sawyer. "And Tom?" asks I.

"Became a fireman not far from here. Raised a brood with Becky Thatcher."

"That right?"

"Sure is."

"Any of them have family around?"

"Mmm," says Orion, "that's a good question. Perhaps some rather removed family, like descendants of second and third cousins to Tom. But the main lines seem to have scattered. As far as Huck, well everything about him is hard to track."

We glanced back at the sketches.

"I best be pushing on," says I.

"It was nice to meet you Mark Finn," says Orion.

"You too," says I. We shook hands.

CHAPTER FOUR

Late that night back at camp, I cooked a couple fish before settling in with Edmond Dantes, the Count. He was holed up in prison, getting tutored by Abbe Faria, and putting in a fair amount of time thinking about home and his loved ones. It got me to thinking. I'd learned a fair bit walking the old neighborhood and visiting the museum. But I still warn't settled on what to do next. Maybe I should push on, thinks I, light out to a place like Montana, which I's told was wild and free and open. Word had it I'd ended up there nohow. Yet something told me to stay, for now.

A few afternoons later I went back into town for another look-see. Not far from where I used to live, I come across a band of boys walking to town. They wore their collars up. I thought about talking to 'em but I just kept a-windin' through the neighborhood sort 'a' aimless.

By and by, jest up the way from the museum, I spotted a little bookstore, in a small, older looking building of slab stone and brick. Now this warn't a common place for me to visit, but, as I say, reading had grown with me. Inside, the place felt cozy, smelled of old, wooden shelves and books, books that looked sort of worn yet timeless. I could relate to that.

I nodded at the attendant as I stepped past the front counter. There warn't hardly anyone inside. Browsing the featured section up near the front of the store, I stopped on occasion to read a blurb on the back of a book. One book was about wives killing their husbands, another on political shenanigans, another about a wild bandit and his illicit drug use. People's interests ain't changed all that much, thunk I. Beyond this section was book-packed shelves lined up to make rows. I found the sports section, then mosied to the westerns, browsing till I found a L'Amour. By chance, I flipped it open to the author bio page. L'Amour stuck these in most his books. It made me smile again reading all the different sorts of jobs he'd held, from lumberjack to elephant handler, seaman to pugilist, military officer to cattle skinner.

With L'Amour in hand, I turned a corner bound for the cashier when a sign highlighting a special "Huck and Tom" section ketched my eye. *Seems like I'm popping up wherever,* chuckled I to myself. I decided to take a gander at the old adventures Tom and I wrote, jest to see what they looked like, you know, on display and for purchase.

I's turning toward the section, when out from behind a row of books steps sunshine itself in a yellow dress. My heart missed a beat, then skipped fast. She had big, blue-green eyes, freckle-speckled cheeks, and the prettiest blonde hair you ever saw. As she walked by, she smiled. I stumbled.

Gathering myself, I continued to the Huck and Tom section. She was heading that way too. I felt clammy and like a frog had lodged in my throat, but in a kind of an exciting way, if you know what I mean. We ended up standing alongside each other. I jest sort of gazed at the Huck and Tom books, feeling stiff and awkward, heart a-thumping.

"Looking for Tom, or for Huck?" asks she, flashing a Mississippi-wide smile.

"Umm, uhh, both."

"Yeah, I suppose that's usually the case. Buy 'em together. I mean, they were bros," she said, laughing a little and putting her fist out to dap, like the Musketeers would do. I was still sorta froze. She held it there an extra moment. I snapped to and brought my fist up. She dapped it. We smiled.

"Of course," continued she, now motioning toward a copy of the *Adventures of Tom Sawyer.* "They were also pretty goofy. Blood oaths, fake robberies. And how about the cartwheels and other shenanigans Tom did just to get Becky's attention?" *At least she's talking about Tom*, thinks I. She added, "He had no clue."

I laughed a little and then cleared my throat. "He did, though, ultimately win Becky's hand. You've got to admit that."

She paused a moment before saying, "You've got a point."

"I also must admit," said she, looking at the back cover of the book, "I don't think I've ever actually read the whole thing, or all of Huck for that matter." She leaned in and in a quieter voice said, "They kind of ramble a little."

I smiled but felt stiff still.

"Are you prepping for the contest?" asked she. I didn't know that of which she spoke.

"No." I glanced at the western I had in-hand. "Had a hankering for Louis L'Amour and thought I'd have a look-see at these Tom and Huck characters."

"Had a hankering, did you?" asked she. "I don't hear that word too often. I like it. Who's L'Amour?"

"Writes Westerns," says I.

"I love Westerns," says she. "I read all the *Little House on a Prairie* books. So good." She paused a moment before nodding toward the book she had in hand. "I'm getting the third *Hunger Games*, which in a way is also a Western. I mean, what American adventure writing isn't, right?" She chuckled a little and sort of fake-punched me on my shoulder.

"Yeah," says I, not sure exactly what in the 'ell she was talking about.

"Have you read *True Grit?*"

"No, I'm jest sort of getting started on Westerns," says I.

"It's good. Powerful female heroine in that one." She paused a moment. "Sorry, my name is Lucy Thoreau," says she, sticking out her hand.

"I'm Mark," managed I as we shook. "Mark Finn."

"It's a pleasure to meet you, Mark. And it's nice to meet you in a bookstore, one of my favorite places in the whole world. Do you live around here?"

"Out in the country a little," says I, nodding toward the direction of Pap's cabin.

"And where do you go to school?"

"Homeschooled," stretched I.

"Oh, nice. Seems so romantic, pastoral, to home-school. Do you like it?"

"I suppose so."

"Where are you from?"

"The bottom of Arkansaw."

"The bottom of Arkansaw?" asks she. She looked a little puzzled. "Do you mean the southern part?"

"That's right."

"That's a neat way to say it."

I warn't about to explain that my mish-mashed vocabulary came from being brung up in long-ago days, mixed with learning the Musketeers' ways, combined with reading westerns and now living at Pap's. Instead I jest nodded and said, "I hear that from time to time. I guess my brain sort of treats words like you might food at one of them meals during which you slosh all the stuff together, meat, stuffing, potatoes, gravy, all of it."

She stared at me for a moment with that puzzled look again. Then she smiled and said, "Well, it's good to meet you, Mark from the bottom of Arkansaw. Take care now."

I could only nod as she turned toward the front of the store. I wanted to say something but that frog got me again. She took a few steps before turning back and saying, "Hey?...Some of us are playing Capture the Flag out near the old graveyard this evening. Good way to meet people. You want to join us?"

Now from my time in Rolling Dunes I knew about Capture the Flag—only I didn't know nothin' about playing it near a graveyard, what with the prospect of stirring up spirits and the like. But I wanted to see Lucy Thoreau again.

"Sure," says I.

"See you then," says she with a smile. Then she was off.

—

Turned out, those collars-up boys I'd seen earlier in the day was out for Capture the Flag that night. They was standing in a group as I approached, still in polos.

"Hey there, what's your name?" one of 'em asked as I got close.

"Mark Finn," says I. "And you?"

"Parker-Wallace," says he, tall and broad-chested. I judged him the leader of the group. "What are you up to?" asked he.

"Oh, nothing really," says I, spotting Lucy and a couple friends of hers up ahead, setting on some swings.

"You know them?" asked Parker-Wallace.

"A little," says I.

"Well, we know most everyone in these parts," he said, motioning toward his friends, all of whom nodded. "But I've never heard of you."

"Ah, don't worry about it; not too many know of me no way."

I started walking over to Lucy and her friends.

"No way?" asks Parker-Wallace. "It's anyway."

"Nice shoes," says another.

Original, thinks I.

As I approached the swing set, a couple other boys came a-walking up along the sidewalk from the other direction. They got to Lucy and her friends jest before I did. They all was greeting each other when I stepped up.

"Hello there, Mark," says Lucy, her smile shining right through the darkness. She introduced me to everyone. Her girlfriends seemed all right, and I liked the cut of the boys' jibs. One of 'em, Randy, reached out to shake hands. "Nice to meet you, Mark," says he.

"Likewise," says I. Jimmy done the same.

By and by Parker-Wallace and his group of boys and another group of girls come over, and we all huddled up to pick sides. Lucy and I got picked to different teams. But the Randy fellow ended up on my team. The two teams huddled separately to plan where to put their flag and how to go about finding the other team's. Then the game was afoot.

While hunting the other team's flag, I hoped to come upon Lucy and strike up a conversation. Only I didn't get much of a chance, between her walking around with a couple girlfriends and what with Parker-Wallace and a buddy hogging time, trying to steal her attention.

'Tis a good thing nohow, reckoned I, seeing as I didn't have no experience to speak of in talking with a girl. Sure, I'd had a crush before, on Mary Jane and Beverly Jean, both of whom ended up having sand, but in those instances our ages didn't match-up and neither was a like scenario. This was different. But the idea of really talking to Lucy Thoreau, as much as I wanted to, struck a new kind of fear in my heart. Some things come easy to me, like reading people's faces, fishing, running back kicks. But not this. To boot, even with our ages matching up, the odds looked long, what with me being sort of lowdown and unlearned and not from these times. Plus, how could I explain to her things that might arise, like why Dr. Knotts and his crew was after me, let alone who I really was?

As for the flag, it warn't too hard to figure where it lay on account of the way the other team fanned itself out and responded to a couple forays from my team. And luckily it warn't in the actual graveyard. I warn't trying to stir up no spirits. After scouting about and observing, I decided the way to get to the flag was from above. So, on the sly, I clumb a tree and moved from it to another, way up high, making little noise, watching below. I jest needed to scoot over to one more tree which would allow me to drop down right next to a shin-high rock, under which I was sure they'd placed the flag. Felt a little shaky high up, stretching from one branch to the next, but I managed. When I dropped down, still unnoticed, I was maybe a fathom from the rock. On the quick, I dashed to it. A couple boys spotted me and hollered, "Stop him, run!" But they was too late. I reached the rock and pushed it aside, revealing the flag, which I grabbed and held high.

"Damn," one of the boys said, rushing in.

Randy, jogging up, declared, "How about that, it's Spiderman!"

Parker-Wallace looked ornery.

"Did I see you drop down out of a tree?" asked Randy. I just shrugged. "Peter Parker stuff right there," says he.

We played one more round, but I didn't find an opening to talk with Lucy until everyone was pushing off. She was guiding her bike along a sidewalk, chatting with her friend Jessica. A-walking by, I gave Lucy a wave. She waved back and said, "Glad you came out, Mark."

She continued walking with her friend. Finally, I thawed. "I'm heading that way, too," said I. "What'd you say I walk with you all?"

"Sure," she said.

When I got abreast of 'em, Lucy introduced Jessica. The sidewalk sloped upward as we walked along, the air crisp, stars a-shining, moon a-glowing.

"So how did you two meet?" asks Jessica.

"At the bookshop," says Lucy. "I was supposed to get Tom Sawyer but somehow I came out of there with the third *Hunger Games*," she said, shrugging. "My mom wasn't happy."

"Oh yeah," said Jessica. "My Mom's trying to get me to read Tom Sawyer, too. I told her I already read it. I'm not reading it again. Anyway, we all know you or Charlotte are going to be Becky."

"Don't be ridiculous," says Lucy.

"It's you or Charlotte," Jessica said again. "Stacey has an outside shot because of her music. Adults love the violin. Then there's always kind of like that fourth, outlier finalist. But that person usually doesn't win."

Lucy shook her head.

"And when you win," continued Jessica, "You'll get paired with Parker-Wallace. And your families will be delighted. And you'll get married."

"Stop it," said Lucy, giggling.

"He's cute. You can learn to like him."

"You're unbelievable."

"Maybe Sterling Lewis. Maybe you and Sterling. Either way, whichever it is, they can propose to you and you two can plan to be married." The two laughed. I wasn't really picking up on what they was getting at exactly. I mean, were they serious?

"It's absurd, isn't it. Tom Sawyer proposes to Becky Thatcher on their first day together. What type of idiocy is that?"

"Different times," Jessica said, smiling.

"Then Tom lets it slip that he'd been engaged once before," says Lucy.

"Moron," says Jessica.

Note to self, thinks I. *Do not propose to Lucy too soon.*

Jessica turned to me. "So Mark, where are you from?"

"Up thataway, in the country a bit," says I, motioning my arm northward.

"Do you go to our school? I don't think I've ever seen you."

"No, I'm homeschooled. My mam and pap is a little different that way."

"Do you have any siblings?" Lucy asked.

"Three brothers and three sisters," whaled I, conjuring a big family for some reason.

"That's awesome," says Lucy.

Near the top of a hill, we made it to Jessica's. She said her goodbyes and went inside then Lucy and I walked on.

"My house is close," said she, looking ahead. "To the top of this hill, then a right and down a little."

We walked in silence a bit.

"So how about you?" asked I. "Do you have siblings?"

"I have two younger sisters. I have some cousins that live in town, too, and other family. My parents grew up here."

We made it to the top of the hill and upon picking up a new street to our right quickly found ourselves in front of a powerful big home with an impressive stone drive. A sign out front read: Rockcliffe Mansion. 'Twas a commanding, three-story structure, built on a shelf of limestone. A cupola set atop the third level and on one side of the home was a huge porte-cochere, supported by columns of the type you find in books on ancient Rome. I must've been gawking, because Lucy said, "Have you ever seen it before?"

"Um, uh, well, like I say, we recently come up from the bottom of Arkansaw, and I don't get to town too often."

"Isn't it incredible?" asks she.

I nodded.

She quick-glanced around and then took me by the arm, "You've got to see the view it gives of town."

We scooted across a sweeping lawn, then along a long row of bushes, till we reached the edge of the limestone shelf upon which the Rockcliffe sat. Out below this high cliff was a splendid view. We could see the whole town of St. Petersburg and the Muddy beyond. We stood there awhile, not saying anything, jest enjoying the view. A flood of memories rolled through me.

By and by Lucy nudged me and we headed back across the lawn, out to the street. Shortly thereafter, we come to Lucy's house. It was big, too, and impressive in its detail. Warn't as large as the Rockcliffe, mind you, but did have three levels and a wide porch which run along the front and swept down the sides. A clutch of sugar maples and oaks sort of stood guard.

At the drive, Lucy said, "Thank you for walking me home, Mark, very gentlemanly."

As she stepped up to the porch, I thunk, *There goes royalty.*

CHAPTER FIVE

The next several days at Pap's passed ruther uneventfully. Explored the forest, fixed up the cabin, read, checked my lines at night, washed up. But whatever I's doing, my mind couldn't shake Lucy Thoreau. Didn't hardly know her of course, but that didn't seem to matter.

When the weekend rolled in, I walked to town again, hoping to get lucky and bump into Lucy. This time when I got to town it warn't as shocking, naturally, to find that they'd put Becky Thatcher's old home on Hill Street as well as Grant's old store and the like. Still, it's not something you get used to. I had it in mind to put in time at the museum. Only, as I come upon it, I see there was a considerable line snaking out of it. In this line was kids that seemed about my age, many of 'em standing with a parent. The line warn't moving fast. I's about to peel off and find something else to do, maybe explore the nearby caves that Tom and the rest of the gang and I used to run, when luck struck and I spotted Lucy in line up ahead. Her father, I presumed, was with her. He wore a sharp suit and a fine hat. *If she's in line, I should probably get in line, too,* thought I. So I slid into the back of it, maybe thirty people or so behind Lucy.

I tapped the shoulder of the boy in front of me. As he turned toward me, I recognized him from Capture the Flag, but I couldn't recall his name straight away.

"What exactly are we standing in line for?" asked I.

He appeared puzzled by my question, like he was wondering if I was playing with a full deck. I jest shrugged my shoulders.

"Well," the boy says, "I'm standing in line to sign-up for the Tom and Becky contest, but I can't really say for sure why you are in line."

"Oh, yeah, that's right. I don't know what I was thinking, the Tom and Becky contest," says I. "I'm doing that, too."

"You're Mark, right?"

"Yes."

"My name's Randy," says he, holding out his hand. "I met you the other day at Capture the Flag."

"Yeah, I remember."

"Nice to meet you again, Mark. You're new to St. Petersburg, right?"

"In a way," says I.

He chuckled a little and shook his head, like I'd mixed him up.

"Um, uh, it's hard to explain," I added. "But basically, yes, I'm new now."

"Well, welcome back, then," says he.

Eager to guide the conversation away from my background, and seeing as I hadn't a clue as to what the Tom and Becky contest was, I said, "It should be one heckuva contest, huh?"

"I'd say. I mean, look at this line—a whole slew of folks have come downtown to put their name in."

"Yeah, the Tom and Becky contest. It sure is something," says I, trying to think of a way to get more info. "Probably take all night, huh?" stabbed I. "You know, to sort through it all and get the winners."

Randy looked at me like I warn't fishing with hooks.

Shrugging again, I motioned toward the line, which had stretched out behind Randy and I, and said, "Well, look at all these people,"

Randy shook his head. He put his hand to his chin before asking, "Wait a minute, you really have no idea what this is, do you?" asks he. "Were you just aiming to visit the museum and got in line? Because if that's the case you can go around all these people."

"No, nah, well, you're sort of right in saying I don't know much about the contest," admitted I. "But I was thinking maybe I should get in it, seeing all these folks. Seems sort of interesting."

"It is pretty interesting, in more ways than one," says Randy, chuckling a little. "Are you in the eighth grade?"

"Happen to be."

"As long as you're in the eighth grade and you live in the district, you're good to go. It's a longer contest than one day though, just letting you know. It's like many weeks long. Today is just sign-up day."

I nodded.

"Where are you from again?" Randy asked.

"I jest moved out this way from the bottom of Arkansaw. So I really don't know much about how this contest works. But I do know a thing or two about Tom Sawyer and Becky Thatcher, I can tell you that."

"All right, well, to give you a little background, every year the town of St. Petersburg puts on a contest to crown a Tom Sawyer and a Becky Thatcher."

"How do you mean?" asks I.

"What do you mean, 'How do you mean?' First, with all due respect, did you know that you have a funny way with words?"

"I feel the same about a lot of you all."

Randy smiled at that. "Here's the deal," he explained. "Each year, one boy and one girl—through a series of competitions: writing an essay, giving a speech, and similar such—wins the distinction of being Tom or Becky for the year. If you win, you represent the town at all kinds of events: ribbon-cuttings, fancy dinners, parades, fairs— here and in other parts of the country. There's word of an international trip this year. They've done that in the past. One year Tom and Becky went to India, another to Australia, I think. People say this year the winners will be sent to China. You get to miss school a lot, too, which is a big draw."

Jessica, Lucy's friend, had said on our walk after Capture the Flag that she thought Lucy was gonna win Becky. Made sense now. Who knows, reckoned I, perhaps I have a shot at Tom. The whole thing sounded bully to me provided it was me and Lucy that was traveling the world as Tom and Becky. And it seemed like the type of contest—acting as if I was Tom Sawyer—that I could get some show in. I mean, I once tricked Tom's own Aunt Sally into thinking that I was Tom Sawyer hisself.

Same time, figured I, it'd be ruther tricky to go for Tom while also trying to lay low, as I'd been a-doing. Maybe I should forget about it, questioned I. How am going to avoid Dr. Knotts and the govment and be Tom Sawyer? 'Cept then I looked up ahead and saw Lucy a-standing in line again, beautiful as can be, and I jest knew that she was gonna be Becky. *Huck, says I to myself, you can't jest hide-out the whole rest of your years. You got to be Tom.*

———

The line moved slow, but I had Randy to chew the fat with. He seemed a right sort, was plenty friendly and didn't hold no airs. And he knew a whole lot about the town and the people in it.

By and by he leaned in and said, "I'm guessing you don't know who the frontrunners for Tom and Becky are?"

"Not really," says I, talking low as well.

He pointed ahead of the line a bit, toward that Parker-Wallace fella. "He's a contender." Randy spoke even quieter. "His dad's a banker. Mom's from old money, tight with members on the Tom and Becky committee. Parker-Wallace butters up the teachers. I think they know he's full of it, but they don't say it. His parents will make sure he's up to speed on the history of the town and Tom Sawyer and all the rest. Vegas would probably put him in the lead. He's unbearable."

I recalled the Musketeers referencing Vegas when talking about college football.

Randy nodded ahead. "The boy next to Parker-Wallace, that's Sterling Lewis. He has a good shot at winning, too. Dad's a prominent lawyer. Passes muster on looks. Pretty smart. Not as snooty as Parker-Wallace. He could definitely win, but Parker-Wallace's parents have more juice."

"How 'bout the Beckys?" asks I.

"See the girl in the red dress near the front of the line, pretty tall?" asked he, pointing toward where Lucy stood. I spotted the girl he spoke of. "That's Charlotte Witherspoon. Her parents own a bunch of McDonald's here and in the adjoining county. She's convinced half the teachers she's the greatest. She's not. Most of the other girls are afraid of her. But this could end up helping her. She can knock 'em off their game. I doubt she knows anything about Becky Thatcher or Tom Sawyer.

But to be fair few of us do. I mean, most of us have read Tom Sawyer but I wouldn't be surprised if she had someone else read it for her. Have you read Tom Sawyer?"

"Yeah," says I.

"What'd you think?"

"It was good but also, you know, he ain't against whaling."

Randy chuckled. "Now Charlotte," continued he, "will get tutoring and probably be able to act like an expert before the contest is through. She wants Becky for her college applications. Schools love it. She's aiming for Harvard or Yale. Her parents are having her do the whole play an obscure instrument thing, too."

I didn't know what in the 'ell he meant by that.

He continued. "Charlotte pretty much runs the cool-girl clique, sets the tone on style. You'll see. Take a look at her dress, her hair, her makeup. It's a little strong, nearly overdone, I'd say, but still oddly effective. Have you ever seen *Mean Girls?*"

"No," says I.

"She could've been in that. I get along with her because, well, I tend to get along with most girls and, you know, I'm into style: hair, clothes, shoes. Girls get me. I get them. But she could've been in that movie. She's basically in that movie."

"You're into style?" asks I, still talking low.

"Oh yeah. Can't you tell?" asks he, as he raised his arms a little and gazed down at his outfit, which consisted of a sport coat over a fancy t-shirt, and some ruther tight-fitting pants. Really, it all seemed pretty tight-fitting; looked ruther smothery.

"Clean lines, Hamptonsy, earthy tones. Sharp fit, right?" asks he.

"I think so," nodded I.

Randy seemed bemused by my response. He pointed his toes upward and looked down at his shoes, which was made of yellow leather. "A little flair with the shoes. I love shoes, which is another reason I get along swimmingly with girls."

He looked me over. I was wearing those moccasins, a pair of my cut-off cargo pants, and a long sleeve under my Rolling Dunes football jersey. The jersey had a tear near the bottom on account of it being pulled on during a game.

"My style?" asked I.

"Oh my," says Randy. "You're kind of like bluegrass Americana meets the frontier meets Walmart. To be honest, I've never seen anything like it. The moccasins take it to another level. Somehow it kinda works, though, which I don't really understand. And the fact that you seem entirely oblivious makes it even more intriguing."

I shook my head and laughed. Generally, I understood about half of whatever it was Randy spoke of.

"My favorite to win Becky is Lucy Thoreau," said Randy, leaning in, still trying to keep his voice low. "Classy. Elegant. Not mean. Actually nice. She has a real shot. She's smart, too. Dad's a judge. Parents are well-connected. The Thoreaus may not be ruthless enough for her to win, however."

This competition sounded like all-out war.

———

A half hour had run along before we made it to the front of the line. Lucy'd left by then. I warn't sure if she'd even seen me.

Two ladies sat at the registration table. Randy stepped up to one of 'em, while I waited on the other. Randy got asked a couple questions and then he showed an I.D. Snap, thinks I, everyone wants papers these days. The Tom in front of me finished up and the registration lady motioned for me to step forward.

"I'd like to put in for Tom," says I.

"Sounds good," says she. "And what's your name darling?"

"Mark Finn," says I.

"Do you have your student I.D.?"

"No ma'am."

"Do you have your birth certificate?"

"Like, for you to keep?"

"Just a copy," said she.

I had the real one—well, the real fake one that Ned had made for me back in Rolling Dunes. I didn't aim to part with that.

"Not right now," says I.

"You'll have to get a copy to us by week's end."

"I can do that."

"Okay, how about your address, what's your address?"

"Mmm, thing is, we're moving," says I. "Do you want my address right now or after we move, which should be tomorrow?"

She looked flabbergasted.

"Which school do you go to?" asked she.

"Uh, well, I'm homeschooled."

"Okay." She took a deep breath. "No problem. We accept homeschooled students. Here's what we'll do, Mark. I'll give you the paperwork and you and your mom or dad can fill it out and bring it back in. Remember, include a copy of your birth certificate. Got it?"

I nodded.

"And we'll need your parents to fill out this form." She handed me another sheet of paper. "I'll put you down for now. Orientation is next Sunday, at the B&B main theater, just a building over [she pointed its direction], six p.m. Make sure you get everything in by the end of day Friday. You can give the forms to the folks working at the theater or slide 'em in the mail slit."

"Yes'm," says I. "Thank you."

I slipped out of there quick, hoping to avoid any more questions.

CHAPTER SIX

Needing a think, I went a-walking about the town. It was a nice day, the sun a-shining. I walked a good ways. By and by, on the edge of town in a little clutch of forest, I sat down, slid off my moccasins, and leaned against a tree to rest and think about this here Tom and Becky contest.

After a while, I got up and walked some more. Found myself near the caves Tom Sawyer and me and the rest of our gang used to have the run of. I wove toward one of the old entrances, planning to walk right in. Only as I approached I noticed a booth out in front with a gaggle of folks standing nearby. There was a sign, no fooling, which read: Cave Entry $8. Stopped me cold. *They're charging people to go into the caves,* marveled I. *Imagine that.* Not even Tom Sawyer would've dreamt up such a thing.

Now, I ain't for paying to go into caves, 'specially caves I've been inside of for free plenty of times, caves about which I knew more than most anyone else. So I peeled off and slid back into the forest, till I found the rocky outcropping I was looking for. I scaled it, then hiked across a stretch of forest which sloped downward a bit. Near the bottom part of this slope was a waist-high boulder. Years back it covered a rock slit which gave access to the network of caves below. With some effort, I moved the boulder jest enough to reveal the slit.

I wiggled through and slid into the cave, climbing down a patch of rock along one side before letting go and dropping several feet to the ground. The air felt nice and cool, as expected. No matter the time of year, 'tis always the same temperature in them caves. That's one of the magical things about 'em. I sat a minute and gazed at the rocky ceiling above, the smooth granite, the shiny obsidian. Still a good place to find some solitude, says I to myself—and to get lost in if need be.

This branch of the cave network sloped downward, and I was reacquainting myself with its nooks and crannies, turning down a branch here another corridor there, when I heard some voices. I followed the voices. After some weaving, I saw up ahead a group being guided along by a lady. Stepping a bit closer, I could hear her describing features of the cave. I's about to turn back and explore on my own when, lo and behold, peering through the dimness, I noticed that Lucy Thoreau was in this group, no whaling. I moved closer. 'Twas her, no doubt, with her pap and her mam. Inching closer, I seen Parker Wallace, too, collar up, with his parents as well, I presumed. Two other families was with them. I trailed while their guide led 'em to another branch of the cave.

Hiding behind a ledge of rock, I overheard the guide say they'd reached the spot at which Tom and Becky encountered all of those bats. Some in the party looked up nervously at the ceiling, crouching like they was getting ready to duck. The guide told 'em not to worry, that naturalists had resettled the bats to a different part of the cave network.

I expected the group to continue working its way in the same direction. But of a sudden the guide said they'd reached the end of the tour, and she promptly walked right through the group and started 'em back from where they'd come. So now they's suddenly coming right for me. I had to think fast. Ruther than have 'em come upon me and spot me behind the ledge of rock, I popped out from my spot and started walking right for them, playing matters cool and natural. I waved hello as I passed 'em and said, "How do you do?" and kept going, like I was jest out for a stroll. The guide looked quite startled, then puzzled. But she didn't say anything as I walked by. She just lifted her lantern a little, with a confused look on her face. Finally, after I'd walked full through the group, she said, "Hey there, where did you come from?"

"Oh, sorry miss, didn't mean to startle," says I. "I went ahead of my group, been to this cave a thousand times."

"Oh, okay," says she. "Well, please join us on our way out and you can reconnect or meet them at the main entrance. You're not supposed to walk through the caves alone."

"Alright," says I, easing into the back of the group. Parker-Wallace sort of smirked at me. Lucy shot me a smile. "Hi, Mark," says she. The guide continued on, explaining away.

"Do you two know each other?" Lucy's mom asked through the semi-lit darkness.

"Yes," says Lucy.

"From school?"

"No, just from 'round town, ma'am," says I. "I'm home-schooled."

"Oh," says Mrs. Thoreau. "And what was your name again?"

"Mark Finn," says I.

"I'm Mrs. Virginia Thoreau," says she, quite proper-like. She wore a dress, which looked nice but didn't make much sense for to go into a cave with. "This is my husband, Robert."

"Hello, Mark," says he, still in his suit from earlier when I saw him and Lucy in line for Becky. "Where are you from?"

"Bottom of Arkansaw," says I.

"The bottom of Arkansaw?" asks he.

"Yes sir. Born on a farm out thataway."

"Did I see you earlier?" asks he, looking me over best he could given the darkness.

"Perhaps," says I. "I put in for Tom. Becky ain't for me." I meant that to be funny, but Mr. Thoreau and his wife just sort of stared at me. Lucy smiled.

We were continuing back through the cave now.

"I met Mark in the bookstore downtown," said Lucy. "The Tom and Huck section."

"That so," said her Mom. "Lucy was supposed to be buying *Tom Sawyer.*"

The grownups walking a little ahead chuckled at that.

"Have you read it?" Lucy's mom asked me.

"Sure," says I. "Good tale. Of course it's chock-full of stretchers. Tom Sawyer did more whaling than Thomas Nickerson hisself."

Lucy's Mam and Pap glanced at each other. Nickerson isn't well known in these times, I noted to myself. Lucy's parents sort of shuffled ahead of us, thankfully. The rest of the group was shuffling along, too.

Lucy trailed a bit behind her parents, which I appreciated. I stepped alongside her.

"Come here often?" asks I.

"Not really," says she, smiling. She nodded ahead. "My parents have some friends in town who are also friends with the Wallaces. They wanted to show their kids the caves."

I looked ahead to their kids. They was on their phones.

"Looks like they're missing the caves," I whispered.

"Yeah, they live on their phones," Lucy said quietly. "Do *you* come here often?"

"Used to," says I. "It's a nice place to have a think, stay cool. And hide out if need be."

"Do you need to hide out a lot?" Lucy asked, half-playing.

"I mean, in case you need to hide out, you know."

"I mean, I guess," she said, laughing a little.

Parker-Wallace, having slow-walked till we came up alongside him, cut in: "Dude, do you just hang out in caves or what?"

"Sometimes."

"Are you like a bat?"

"Parker!?" Lucy said.

"I'm not trying to be rude. I'm just saying, it's odd. I don't know many people who wear moccasins and hang out in caves."

"Well, I don't know many people who wear their collars up," says I.

Parker-Wallace shrugged. "Did you cut your pant-legs near your calves?"

"Yes."

He shook his head before saying, "I saw you in line to register for Tom and Becky."

Lucy smiled. "That's great, Mark. I didn't see you there, but I guess my dad did somehow."

"I's jest a little ways behind you," says I.

"Well, I don't mean to burst your bubble, Mark," says Parker-Wallace, "but if I were you, I wouldn't waste my time on that. It takes a lot to win the competition. To be

Tom Sawyer you need to do well in school, know how to dress, understand history, all types of things."

"Tom Sawyer warn't strong in none of them categories," says I. "Other than perhaps knowing the history of a band of pirates or a den of thieves."

"I just don't want you to waste your time, and I don't think you're Tom Sawyer quality," said he.

"Stop it," Lucy said.

"Well, I'm being honest," said Parker-Wallace. "Isn't that better than having him waste time?"

We'd come to the spot at which I'd dropped into the cave. I didn't want to have to explain to any of the workers up near the main entrance how I'd ended up with Lucy's group. So I up and said, "Lucy, I gotta go. I look forward to seeing you at the Tom and Becky competition."

Right quick, I stepped to a sidewall and clumb about eight feet up, to crouch on a side outcropping of cave rock. From there I pulled myself through the crevice I'd used to drop in. When I peered back down through the crevice into the cave, I saw Lucy and Parker-Wallace staring up back at me, wide-eyed. *My, she's beautiful,* thinks I.

———

I hiked a good stretch from there, looping my way about, mostly through forest, steady upward, till I found myself approaching Lover's Leap.

Set high atop a powerful tall limestone bluff, Lover's Leap gives sweeping views of St. Petersburg. Only 'tisn't so easy to get to the edge of the bluff no more without which you gotta jump a fence that some fool put up. At the edge of the bluff, I looked out to my left and saw farmland above the forest in which Pap's cabin set. Below the forest was the town. And winding along it all was the Muddy. Straight downward from this bluff, about two Mark Twains below, was train tracks. They ran across a sort of rocky, earthy outcropping of raised riverbank which sloped downward from the tracks for the length of a football field or so to the river. Up ahead, the tracks run alongside town. All in all, 'twas a mighty fine view.

Standing there a-gazing, I heard the town clock chime in a new hour and heard the blare of a train's horn. As the four chimes rung, I watched the rail cars roll by below—first came open-top coal cars, then cattle and seed cars, and finally flatbeds with big ole round hay bales strapped to 'em, three bales per flatbed.

By and by I hopped back over the guard fence, fitting to push on, when I noticed a little display they'd put up to describe Lover's Leap. It told of the centuries-old legend which holds that a young Indian lady from this side of the river fell for a warrior who belonged to a forbidden tribe from across the river. Her pap and the rest of her tribe found out about this. Elders, her father included, told her there would be no show with the man she'd fallen for. They tried to force her to marry a different man, one from her tribe whom she despised. Instead of complying, she came to the edge of this here bluff and leapt to her death. Hence the name.

However, the display told, there is another version of the legend. This one holds that the man with whom she'd fallen in love followed her to the bluff and called to her jest before she jumped. When she turned and saw him, hope rose back to her heart. The two lovers embraced and decided to escape, to live out their lives together far away from there. Only they'd been pursued by warriors from her tribe, including the young man she'd refused to marry, and they were fast approaching. The lovers could not go back the way they'd come. They were looking down in anguish when, by wild happy chance, along the dirt-packed riverbank road below, they saw a farmer coming along, guiding a team of four horses pulling a wagon. And what do you know but the wagon was filled with hay. The lovers looked back at their pursuers, then knowingly at each other, took each other by the hand, and leapt. They hit the hay hard but was none the worse for wear. And the four horses pulling that wagon, spooked by the sudden jolt of the two lovers, took off as if shot out of a cannon. Those horses kept a-running, too. By the time they finally stopped, the lovers were in the clear. Word is, they continued westward, claimed a settlement, made a farm, and raised a happy brood.

Some say neither version is true, that instead an upstart newspaperman made the whole thing up for show back in the 1800s. Something like a fella I once knew, Clemens, might do. The story had always sounded like a whale to me, people going to all that trouble over romance. But looking out another time from Lover's Leap, knowing the kinds of powerful things that was stirring within me when it come to Lucy Thoreau, I saw how maybe 'twas possible that the two had landed on that wagon and headed West, left alone to build their lives.

CHAPTER SEVEN

On my way back to Pap's, something nudged me toward the Tom and Huck Museum. Next I knows I was back inside it, looking at old photos, reading old yarns, thinking about old times.

Orion Halley, that older man with the wild-looking silver hair which sort of shoots straight up, had greeted me when I arrived. He let me in no charge. While I browsed, he went about closing up the place.

By and by he came up to me. I was looking at a rendering of Jim and I on our raft at night.

"I like to think of all the stars they could see back then from their raft, in the deep of the night on the quiet stretches of river," says Orion.

"Me too," says I.

I took a few steps over to the next display on the wall and found a description of myself written by Mark

Twain, that fella I mentioned who I knew growing up, who ended up writing for newspapers in and around St. Petersburg, He wrote books, too, like the one in which he took a Connecticut Yankee and threw him in with King Arthur's gang. Anyway, of me, he said: "He was ignorant, unwashed, insufficiently fed; but he had as good a heart as ever any boy had. His liberties were totally unrestricted. He was the only real independent person—boy or man— in the community, and by consequence he was tranquilly and continually happy and was envied by all the rest of us. We liked him; we enjoyed his society. And as his society was forbidden us by our parents the prohibition trebled and quadrupled its value, and therefore we sought and got more of his society than of any other boy's."

"Doesn't sound like a bad way to live, uh?" asks Orion.

"I imagine it'd have its advantages," says I. "But I don't know about being 'tranquilly and continually happy.' Everyone's got their ebbs and flows, jest like the river."

Orion smiled at that. "Yeah, I suppose that's so."

"It sure is something reading up on the old gang, Tom Sawyer and the rest. But some things I just don't know if they got right," says I.

"Really?"

"Don't you think the cabin Huck Finn lived in with his mam and pap was a mite more rickety than the one on display jest down the road there?"

"Well, I'm sure they had to reinforce it, sturdy it up a bit."

"Yeah, I'd wager it warn't jest a mite more rickety, but whole lot more rickety—a place that could make you feel mighty uneasy."

Orion eyed me quizzical-like. "My father used to say something similar," says Orion. "He was born in 1895, his father in the 1850s. He had a pretty full view of St. Petersburg. Maybe you're onto something."

We were quiet for a few moments before Orion says, "You know, you asked me earlier about what happened to Huck. Well, what do you think happened to him?"

"To Huck Finn?" asks I.

"Yes," says Orion.

"Who knows? That story of him ending up in Montana sounds like something that could've happened."

"Yeah, but no one's ever confirmed it," says Orion. "Don't you think that seems a little odd? I mean, how does history lose track of Huckleberry Finn?"

"Maybe he dasn't want to be kept track of," says I.

"Maybe."

He went to lock up the back. When Orion returned, he found me in a kind of nostalgic fog, staring at the life-sized replicas of Jim and me on our raft.

"Time to head out, Mark," said he gently.

Outside, before pushing off, Orion said, "It's been a pleasure talking with you, Mark. If you ever need anything, don't hesitate to ask. All right now?"

I thought of the paperwork for the Tom and Becky contest. Orion Halley seemed like someone I could count on, similar to Coach Rogy, my football coach back in Rolling Dunes. "Um, well, actually maybe there is something you can help me with," said I.

"Sure, what's that?"

"I was wondering if you could make a copy of my birth certificate?" says I. "You see, my mam and pap and me and my siblings, we live out on a farm and my parents like us to keep to ourselves. They would frown upon me putting in for this Tom and Becky competition."

"Say no more," says Orion. He pointed up to a crossstreet. "My house is just up thataway, then to the left. I'll make copies of your birth certificate, and I'll show you a Rube Goldberg machine."

"Rube Goldberg?" asks I.

"Yes. Ever heard of 'em?"

"No," says I.

"They're marvelous, chain reaction-type contraptions, you know, that do simple things in a complex fashion."

"I think maybe on a cartoon I might've seen one," recalled I, thinking of when Johnny MacShea's little brother would watch Saturday morning television.

As we approached Orion's big, old house, he paused a moment and said, "Wait, I want to show you something. Let me step inside, then you ring the doorbell."

"Okay," shrugged I.

When I rung the bell a ruther peculiar thing happened. A wooden cuckoo bird jutted out from a hole in the wall jest above me and started "coo-cooing." It was quiet several moments then I heard what sounded like a gong being struck. Quiet came again for a bit. I stood there bewildered. A deep voice bellowed, "Who goes there?" I started to say my name when a door flung open. There stood Orion Halley, smiling. "It worked!" he said, motioning me inside.

He positioned me in front of a large contraption in the parlor and then stepped back toward the front door, saying, "Now watch from inside."

He stepped outside, pulled the front door shut, and rung the bell. I heard the bird start "coo-cooing" again. And now that I was inside, I could see that the movement of the bird pulled a string which nudged a marble onto a track. The marble circled downward, picking up speed, till it hit a spring which unleashed a lever that whacked a gong. The vibrations of the gong started another marble rolling down a different, steep track at the bottom of which it bumped into a button, triggering that voice to bellow: "Who goes there?"

Orion, having stepped back into the parlor, looked at me excitedly, "It sprung your touch into motion, then that motion to sound, back to motion, touch, and sound. The trick is to get the vibrations of the gong strong enough to move the second marble."

My eyes were wide.

"A functional Rube Goldberg machine," says he. "C'mon, let me show you the place."

He nudged me into the main hall. I noticed that an image of the night sky, with stars aplenty, ran along its ceiling. On my right, we passed by a large, wide living room, with a ceiling that also had a map of stars on it. In the middle of this room sat a big Rube Goldberg machine.

Orion nodded toward it, "I'm not quite done with that one."

Throughout the house there was gadgets and tools here, stacks of books and notebooks there. As we passed by another great room, I spotted a grand piano, an easel stand, and, along a workbench, several old cash registers in various stages of repair.

Orion motioned toward the registers, "Gilded age, made mostly in Ohio. I had a phase during which I collected 'em and tinkered with 'em." He stared blankly at 'em for a second, before saying, sort of absent-mindedly, "I suppose I should finish fixing 'em up."

We reached the kitchen. He must live alone, reckoned I, pulling my gaze upward to an image of a constellation on the ceiling.

"I put Aquarius, the cupbearer, on the kitchen ceiling," explained he.

"Makes sense," says I, smiling.

"Now," says he. "You need a copy of that birth certificate."

He guided me up a couple flights of backstairs to a third floor office. Against one wall of the office was a table, half of which was covered with what appeared to be computer parts. Along another wall, above a workbench, were shelves full of tools and little machine parts. Across from this set a wide desk with papers strewn atop and a computer and a printer.

Seemed like Orion owned every tool and gadget known to man. In time I'd learn a lot of their names. He had monkey wrenches and pipe wrenches, handsaws and mallets, chisels and screwdrivers, wire strippers and soldering irons and scalpels, integrated circuit pin straighteners and chip extractors. And e'ry kind 'a' bolt and nut and washer.

"What do you do in here?" asks I, gazing around.

"Astronomy and shop work, mostly. Tinker with machines, like my telescopes and computers, stuff like that," says Orion.

He showed me a circuit board and computer chips and gave a quick demonstration of a laser cutter. He said he started tinkering as a kid and that he still worked on cars, time to time. Ned—the tech-minded Musketeer from Rolling Dunes—would like this whole set up, judged I.

Orion stepped over to a sliding glass door and motioned for me to step out onto a deck. There a large telescope pointed to the sky. Another, smaller scope, stood beside it.

"You ever study the sky?" asks he, as he looked through the large telescope.

"Yes, sir," says I. "Oftentimes at night when my belly's full or I'm just putting in the time or churning something."

"Have a look through that," says he, moving to the side.

As I gazed through the scope my eyes popped. There were more stars in view than gold coins in the treasure Tom Sawyer and I had found.

"Bully," says I.

"It is, isn't it?" says he. "More stars than grains of sand on Earth. Hard to fathom."

Back inside Orion's office, I noticed on the wall near his desk, a large poster about ten feet wide and stretching floor to ceiling. It was a rendering of a whole slew of stars. And it had all sorts of markings and notes written upon it.

Orion noticed me looking at the poster. "As I say, I'm a skygazer, part of a network of them spread across the globe," says he.

"That so?" asks I.

Waving his hand in a sweeping motion, as if it was crossing the sky, he said, "We use data from telescopes in space, like Kepler, and couple it with our own observations. Just last month, we found two planets in the Goldilocks Zone."

"What's the Goldilocks Zone?"

"Areas of space in which planets, based on their positioning and size and makeup, may very well have the conditions needed to host life." He paused several moments, then added, "Our universe, Mr. Finn, our natural world: it's a gobsmacker."

I agreed; couldn't help but think of how I'd been thawed out a glacier and pumped full of chemicals and eased back to life after decades in a deep arctic freeze.

"Now," says Orion suddenly, "your birth certificate."

He quick-stepped over to the printer. While waiting for it to warm up, he asked if I worked with computers.

"No," says I. "We don't have any out on the farm."

"How 'bout at school?"

"My mam homeschools me. I don't go to school proper."

"Well, good for her," says he.

I pulled from my back pocket the birth certificate and the paperwork given to me at the Tom and Becky registration.

"They've taught you farming though, right?" asked Orion.

"Oh, yeah," says I, fibbing—'bout all I knew of farming was borrowing watermelons from old Bishop's orchard.

"Good," says Orion, eyeing the copy of my birth certificate.

I warn't too worried about it appearing off-note because Ned was like a wizard with his digital conjuring and the certificate had worked back in Rolling Dunes. Still, Orion eyed it ruther close.

"I'll print a few extra just in case," said he finally. While he waited for the printer to warm up, I filled out the paperwork.

Back downstairs, before I pushed off, Orion said, "Quick question for you, Finn. Thing is, last year I bought a little farmland outside of town. I haven't done much with it, but I'm thinking about working it next season. I was wondering if you could help me with this question: when you're planting soybeans, should the rows be four feet from each other or six?"

"Oh, we don't do soybeans," says I, a-wiggling.

"Oh, okay, mmm…well what is it that you all do plant?" asks he.

"Mostly corn, a little hay," says I.

"Fantastic, because that was my other question. I'm thinking about corn, too. I was wondering: would you say keeping each plant about four feet apart sounds right?"

"Sure," says I, a-guessing. "Sounds about right."

"And maybe keep each of the plants in a row about two to three feet apart?"

"Yeah, I think so," says I, trying to picture what a cornfield looks like when first planted. "I pretty much just do what my parents tell me. Haven't thought about it too much."

Orion nodded kinda slowly before asking, "These parents out in the country on this corn and hay farm, they're probably awful busy taking care of everything, huh?"

"Yes, sir," says I.

"Well, I'm in my third floor shop most evenings. Anytime you want to come by, grab some grub, stop on in."

"All right," says I.

"Come to think of it," adds Orion. "I could use some help mapping a sector of stars I'm studying. It's tedious work. But I can pay you hourly, maybe a couple evenings a week. Could use some help time to time with the Rube Goldberg machines, too."

I still had cash from that Notre Dame ticket, but it was running low. "Sure," says I, heading out. "Much obliged."

———

I stopped by the B&B Theater to slide my birth certificate and paperwork into the mail slit.

A-walking to Pap's, I got to thinking about how Orion tinkers with newfangled computers and machines, yet works at a museum full of old stories and dead people. Well, mostly dead people—I mean, I'm alive, of course. He lives in two worlds, judged I, the old and the new. It struck me that I did as well. Only I didn't know nearly as much as I should about the new world. With Dr. Knotts looking for me, the govment, too, I reckoned that learning the new ways could help me stay ahead of my pursuers. Shoot, if it warn't for Ned's tech savvy, I wouldn't've likely been able to break away from that govment facility outside Rolling Dunes.

Technology seemed like witchcraft to me when I first seen it, televisions and smart phones and video games, all of it. But the Musketeers had learned me the basics of how to work with it, and Orion made it seem like something you could get your head around. Working some nights would earn me dough and probably learn me a thing or two, determined I.

Walking onward, I let my mind wander. 'Twas pleasant. The sky was lit jest right by a full moon; the air felt cool and still. And my step had a nice bounce to it on account of knowing that in a few days I'd see Lucy Thoreau at orientation, and from sensing that in Orion I had a new, if ruther unlikely, friend.

CHAPTER EIGHT

Sunday evening, I went to the B&B theater for orientation. In the lobby, people was already checking in. Hopeful that my paperwork had gone through, I stepped up to the registration table and gave my name. The lady smiled, found me on the list, and said, "Welcome to the Tom Sawyer and Becky Thatcher competition, Mark." *Well, what do you know,* thunk I, *they cleared me for Tom.*

I slid into a backrow seat of the playhouse. Seemed like a hundred boys and a hundred girls had shown up. Scanning the seats ahead, I spotted Lucy near the front, with a gaggle of girls around her.

I felt a tap on my shoulder. It was Randy.

"Good to see you," says he.

"Hello, there," says I. He grabbed a seat next to me.

"I didn't think I'd see you here, to be honest."

"That so?"

"Well, I mean, you did ask me what we were in line for the other day?"

"That's true."

'Bout then a Mrs. Hawkins walked to the front of the stage. She welcomed us and thanked the Chamber of Commerce for being the lead sponsor and thanked several companies for their support: Dollar Tree, Wal-Mart, Anta-XT, Dollar General. She explained how the stages of the contest would unfold over the coming weeks: first, eighth grade teachers at the local public and private schools would receive a list of the contestants they teach and then rate them on interpersonal skills, scholastic standing, citizenship, and responsibility. This presented a challenge, realized I, seeing as I didn't have marks, was dodging the govment, and didn't have many responsibilities, other than needing to avoid the govment and Dr. Knotts, oh and generally needing to find my way.

Hope sprung back to my heart when Mrs. Hawkins says, "Now, if you're homeschooled, the teachers won't be able to rate you, of course. So we're going to ask that you get an adult in your life—can't be your parents—to do so."

Orion'll do it, reckoned I straightaway.

After those ratings arrived, a panel of judges would score each of us on a short speech we were to give about why it is we should be either Tom or Becky. A week after that, we'd need to submit an essay on why Tom or Becky matters. The judges would then slosh everything together—ratings, speech, essay—and give each of us an overall score. The top twelve boys and the top twelve girls would stay in the competition. That simple.

Now, if you made it to that final twenty-four, more obstacles awaited before you could expect to be named Tom or Becky. I could worry about that later, reckoned I. For now, I needed to make it among the final twelve boys.

When Mrs. Hawkins finished running through the contest's particulars, a video screen dropped down behind her to show a short film about the actual lives of Tom Sawyer and Becky Thatcher, and of people like Ole Miss Watson and Jim and mine ownself, which was quite awkward. The film aimed to show what life was like back then. It told of the book Tom had written and the one I'd penned, noting how many copies they'd sold since going to print and the like. English class back in Rolling Dunes had learned me most of it, but it was steady surprising to think that so many people read those books. The film spent some time on that fella Twain, too, you know, who helped me a bit with the writing. But, like usual, they fattened his role. Next, the film played up the long history of the Tom and Becky contest, showed images of Toms and Beckys from years prior and of some of the things they'd done—like when the Tom and Becky of one particular year went to France and that of another year went to India. *Either'd be nice to go to with Lucy*, judged I.

Back out in the lobby, Randy and I chewed the fat and lolled a bit. I was hoping to see Lucy, maybe muster the gumption to strike up a conversation with her.

Turns out, I didn't need to seek her out because when she and her friends come out to the lobby and spotted Randy, they came right over. They fussed over him and told him they liked his shoes and then he turned to me and said to the girls, "Some of you haven't met my new friend Mark. He's trying out for Tom, too."

They said hello and gave me a wave or shook my hand. One of them asked where I went to school.

"He's homeschooled," explained Randy.

Another looked at my moccasins.

"It's endearing. You'll see," said Randy.

Randy got to chatting some more with a few of the girls, and by and by I stepped over to Lucy.

"Good to see you," says I.

"You too, Mark. What'd you think of the whole thing?"

"It's gonna be a hoot trying to be Tom," says I.

"I'm excited to see how it all goes," says she. "It's kind of peculiar that it's a competition, though, considering how subjective it seems. Still, it should be fun. That's how I'm looking at it."

"That's a fine view," says I.

A few of her friends were nudging her along. Apparently they aimed to get ice cream. "Well, see you guys later," says Lucy.

Moments later, Parker-Wallace and a few of his buddies walked past. He must've still been smarting over my interaction with Lucy in the cave and had probably jest seen us talking because he looked at me sideways as he walked by. Then he said over his shoulder, "You don't have to dress like Tom Sawyer yet. The competition hasn't even started."

He and his buddies chuckled at that.

"Interesting," Randy said, watching 'em walk through the lobby.

"What?" asks I.

"He thinks you're a threat. Perhaps he's right."

———

After Orientation, I stopped at Orion's. The cuckoo bird and gong and booming voice alerted him to my arrival. He greeted me warmly and guided me to his upstairs office shop; wanted to show me something. We stepped out onto the viewing deck where he had me take a gander through the telescope.

"Do you see that, middle of the view?" he asked.

"Looks like stars."

"Yes, but do you see one that looks a little different?"

"They all pretty much look the same."

"No, no, no," says Orion, nudging me out of the way. He took a quick look through the scope before motioning me back.

"Now," says he, "do you see right in the middle, the four stars close to each other which nearly make a rhombus?"

Rhombus, thinks I, trying to recall my lessons.

"Sort of like a diamond shape," says he, "but lain on its side."

"I think so," says I.

"Alright, now it's a little faint, but near the middle of the rhombus do you see a spot?"

"I do," says I.

"That, my friend, is a recently discovered planet, compliments of a fellow star-gazer in Australia. And this planet appears to possess the Goldilocks zone qualities we talked about."

"You think there's people up there?"

"Well, not likely humans—but who knows? Could be anything out there," says Orion. "Do you think we're alone?"

"Well, I guess, I jest don't know," fumbled I.

"Billions of galaxies," says Orion, waving his arms toward the sky. "The odds that we're alone are astronomically low. Fermi's Paradox."

I didn't know of this Fermi, but I had been fetched out of a glacier. *So who the 'ell knows*, figured I.

"What's Fermi's Paradox?"

"It refers to the puzzling situation we find ourselves in, namely that there is no hard evidence of advanced extraterrestrial life even though the statistical probability for it is high."

"Mmm," says I. "Maybe we jest don't look for it good."

Orion chuckled. "Perhaps."

He started in on the probabilities of there being other life and how the discoveries that skygazers continued to log were making the odds even greater. By and by he took a deep breath and looked at me like he was trying to remember something.

"Rube Goldberg," says he. "Can you help with some elements of my latest machine?"

"Sure," says I.

We headed back downstairs.

"Oh, I'm glad you came," says he, on our way. "But let's get some coffee, first, and some Moon Pie."

We spent most of our time working on technical elements of his latest machine, like bolting an air spout to a board or tightening hinges. We connected a few hoses to valves. Orion taught me how to best use certain tools, like his electric drill. We even constructed a pulley. Worked a good couple hours and he gave my twenty bucks on account of it.

'Fore pushing off, I asked Orion if he could fill out the questionnaire for the Tom and Becky contest, provide an assessment of me in those categories that Mrs. Hawkins spoke of. He agreed to do so. And then he started a-thinking. He has a way of looking absent for a stretch while somewhere deep in his brain he chews something.

"If you're going to go for Tom," says he, "we'll need to make sure you know more about Tom Sawyer—and Becky Thatcher, for that matter—than anyone else in the competition. Even then, odds are it won't matter. Often as not, they pick a kid who comes from a prominent family. Let me give you a little test, for bearings?"

"Fine by me," says I.

"Who's Tom's aunt?"

"Which one? He had two."

"Good answer. Both."

"Aunt Polly and Aunt Sally."

"In which cave did Tom get lost with Becky Thatcher."

"McDougal."

"What name did Tom give to his robber band at the end of the novel?"

"Tom Sawyer's Gang didn't rob nothing other than maybe some sugar cookies. He warn't ever a pirate, neither. Tom Sawyer spun more yarns than a seamstress."

"Who did Tom get off of a bum murder rap?"

"We..." oops, thought I. "I mean, the night in the graveyard Huck and Tom saw that Muff Potter didn't do it."

"Correct," says Orion. "Alright. Now, they'll likely ask for analysis, not just of Tom but the book itself. What is it getting at?"

"Yarn-spinning," says I, "plain and simple. Giving folks a look-see."

Orion laughed at that. "Okay, well, it sounds like you know your stuff. I'll get this paperwork in," says he, with that twinkle in his eye.

That twinkle worried me a little, though, because it was one of them twinkles that made me think he'd figured something out. What it was he'd figured, I warn't sure.

As I started to head out, Orion suddenly stood up like he'd forgotten something, and said, "Wait, follow me."

He rushed ahead of me and out the front door, waving his arms sort of aimlessly. We reached his three-stall garage. He pulled open the door to the first stall.

"Do you want a bike?" asked he, stepping into the garage, glancing around. "I noticed you're walking everywhere."

Several bikes hung on a rack on a side wall and there were bike parts on a workbench along a far wall. In the other two garage stalls sat two cars, each covered by a tarp.

"Here we go," says Orion, pulling off the rack a bike that looked like none of the other kids'.

"The Spacelander," says he, gazing at it like he did the stars. "A balance of art and science with a cosmos motif, blended beautifully into a bicycle."

He rolled it out to the driveway, before adding, "I got it from a friend of mine back in the '60s, in Michigan, when I used to work in the auto industry. A fellow named Benjamin Bowden. Ever hear of him?"

"No. But I've been to Michigan," says I, recalling the time I swum across the U.S.-Canada border.

"Try it out," says he, tilting the bike to me.

I took hold of the handlebar. It was indeed a splendid bike to behold. Problem was, I didn't know how to ride it. Hadn't ever ridden a bike. I tried to think how I might keep Orion from realizing I hadn't ridden one before. He'd probably figure that quite odd, reckoned I.

He must've noticed my hesitation. Because next, he asked, "Have you ever ridden a bike before young man?"

"Well, it's just that, out on the farm we don't have bikes," stretched I.

Orion paused a moment, his eyebrows raised a bit.

"Mmm...uh, uh," says he. "Well, it's not too hard. Just go slow at first. Practice on the driveway. You brake by pushing the wheels backward."

My first few tries made for some wobbliness. I managed to at least catch the pavement with my foot without falling. Orion rolled a cigar and watched while I worked on getting the hang of it. Soon I's rolling up and down Orion's driveway with relative ease.

"You can ride now," says he then, smiling.

"Yes, I can," says I. "Thank you."

He nodded, and I pedaled off.

CHAPTER NINE

About a quarter-mile or so from Pap's, I found a snaggle of brush alongside a big tree in which to hide the
Spacelander. I walked the rest of the way to the cabin and
fell out mighty quick.

Next several days passed ruther uneventful. I fished
the Muddy and the pond off-hours, lolled about, finished
the Count's tale, started in on another L'Amour. Took
walks through the forest, washed in the river, rinsed my
clothes. One night, with darkness deep, I sat outside
the cabin and got to looking skyward and thinking of
Johnny and Ned and Tank and what they might be up
to. And I guessed at what Dr. Knotts and his henchmen
was doing. Figured he had some of 'em out in the North
Atlantic hunting gas and minerals while posing as envi-
ronmentalists, and one or two others hunting my whereabouts. Lucy sprung to my mind, of course: her smile,

her graceful way of moving, her sheer beauty. She had me walloped. I also thought of the upcoming speeches, set for Sunday, that we was to give on why we'd make a good Tom or Becky. Thing is, though, nothing came to me as far as how to tackle it.

On speech day I met the sun late-morn, then headed to town. The Beckys was first, one o'clock, at the B&B Theater. The Toms was at five. I arrived at the theater early, hoping to ketch Lucy's speech. About a quarter of the way through the Beckys, Randy shown up and took a seat next to me.

He knew each girl that stepped on stage to perform, and he filled me in on 'em. This one did well in school, another not so much. This Becky run fast with the boys, another one slow. This one was pleasant as can be, another pretentious. In between the Beckys' performances, he gave me the skinny on the judges. Four of 'em sat in the first row of the theater, a-watching, while the fifth judge, Mrs. Hawkins, was on stage and would call each Becky up to perform.

"The judge in the naked sweater," Randy said, nodding toward the judge's row, "that's Mrs. Brown."

"Naked?" asks I.

"It's a color," says Randy, smiling. "Like beige."

"Oh, okay."

He motioned again toward the judges. "Anyway, Mrs. Brown teaches at the middle school. No style. Quite bland. But she's well-liked. Solid judge. I would love to give her a makeover."

Another Becky started her speech. We listened. Hers went a lot like the others: listing accomplishments, a note on earning high marks, and talk of activities, like golf or tennis or showing horses. When this particular girl finished explaining why she'd make a good Becky, Randy leans in and says, "Mrs. Klein is the judge with the yellow sweater. She runs the Women's Club and is on the board at the Chamber of Commerce. Husband owns an engineering firm. Not hurting for money. Heard she plays a lot of cards. Bridge. Classic Northeastern style, high-end sweaters, sometimes with a brooch. Fine watches. Attention to detail. Impressive but not my thing. Sometimes she actually carries a Lightship basket as a purse. I think she got it at the Vineyard, maybe Nantucket. That's where the Kleins vacation."

I had not an inclination of what he spoke.

"Mr. Testa," he continued, pointing ahead to another judge, "grey sweater. He's a real estate developer. Recently divorced, recently remarried. Married some gal like twenty years younger than him. Wears those Italian button-ups, leaves one button too many undone. Lotta chest hair action. Gold chain. He motorcycles now, you know, tools around in a chrome-laden Harley. Used to seem as if he hung with the elite set. But lately he's acted like a total wild card. Fun personality. Hard to predict.

'Next to him is Mr. Smullens," Randy continued. "Teaches at the local college, economics. Offers a college-level intro course at my sister's high school, too. She takes it. She's not a fan. He's quite smug. The kind of guy that just knows better. Wouldn't be caught dead at a Dollar General but is a principal investor in all three of the county's Dollar Generals. Comes from money. Family used to be co-owners of the shoe factories in St. Petersburg, ages ago. Style is higher-end established, think Ralph Lauren, Hilfiger. Fancies himself quite worldly. Went to Yale. Do you know how you know someone went to Yale?"

"No."

"They told you." Randy chuckled at his own joke.

We listened to another Becky who sounded a lot like the one we'd just heard. Randy nodded ahead to the judge on stage who was calling up the Beckys. "That's Mrs. Hawkins," says he. "She teaches at the high school. She's fun. Good energy. Her husband runs a restaurant in town that they own. They have kids who are generally quite normal. Somehow she ended up on the board of the Chamber of Commerce. Probably through the restaurant. She's hot, obviously, and has solid style even though she's a soccer mom. I mean, look at the skirt and blouse and heels. She's a little crazy, but in a good way. I don't think she really knows much about Tom Sawyer or Huck Finn or Mark Twain, but I think she's pretty open-minded and I think she actually likes kids."

I don't know how in the 'ell he knew all this.

"Far as I can tell," Randy said. "Mr. Smullens and Mrs. Klein will vote with established money. Mrs. Brown will be open-minded. Mr. Testa is going through some sort of mid-life crisis. So who knows. Mrs. Hawkins? She'll vote her own way. So if someone's going to beat Parker-Wallace or someone in his circle, they'll have to get Brown, Jones, and Hawkins to vote for them. All three. It's a tall order."

Lucy was called next. She walked up to the stage, back straight, graceful as the sun moving across the sky. She stepped to the microphone, introduced herself, and explained some of her accomplishments. Then her speech got interesting. "But that's not why I should be Becky," says she. "I should be Becky because I can relate to her.

'When Becky first meets Tom in the *Adventures of Tom Sawyer*, she's on a sort of literal pedestal, the front porch, like the stage I'm on now. She's put on a figurative pedestal in the novel as well. She's from an aristocratic family, has a prominent father, and is expected by outsiders to have impeccable properness, unblemished societal marks. As such, her fullness isn't easily understood, even by herself. I can relate. Times have changed since then, of course, and I'm different than Becky, but I can relate to all of that.

'Becky has a keen interest in books, sometimes on topics like anatomy, which at that time was deemed unusual for a society girl. I love books as well. But I don't like books on anatomy or math or science or coding, even though I'm told at school that I should, that girls need to do STEM, STEM, STEM. I like old books, like Jane Austen novels and the *Little House on the Prairie* series. I also like biographies and fantasy and futuristic books, like *Hunger Games*. I don't like people telling me what books I should read, and I don't think Becky did, either.

'By novel's end, Becky proved tougher than most thought. I think people view me as fragile. But I think I'd make a strong Becky Thatcher, one who can genuinely relate to her character, express it well, and represent it well, while still being true to myself. Thank you."

As she walked off the stage, all I could think was: *There goes Becky.*

———

About an hour's more of hopeful Beckys performed speeches, then 'twas the Toms' turn. Up at the podium, Mrs. Hawkins reminded us boys that our essays on why Tom was an important character would be due in one week. Then she called on the first boy to come up.

The Toms ran along a lot like the Beckys, talking up marks and extracurriculars: sports, school govment positions, clubs. Parker-Wallace and Sterling Lewis had a whole list of accomplishments and credentials. Got me wondering how in Cairo I'd get to the final twenty-four.

Pondering it made me nervous. Seemed like there warn't no good way to play it. But then I thought of the Louis L'Amour book I's reading—not so much the yarn itself as the description in it of L'Amour's life. I was still in thought, working the plan out in my mind when Randy nudged me. I looked over at him.

"They called you, Mark. Go up there," he whispered to me, motioning for me to hurry.

I stood up and started for the stage. Mrs. Hawkins set her pen down on the podium and said, "Ah, there you are."

As I say, the four other judges sat in the first row, and as I walked to the stage I passed close by Mr. Testa who was at an end seat alongside the center aisle. I gave him a pat on the shoulder and leaned down to quickly shake his hand and say hello. He smiled a little awkwardly as he hadn't expected me to do this, but he still gave me a hearty greeting. Next, I walked onto the stage, stepped over to shake Mrs. Hawkins's hand, and then made it to centerstage and channeled my inner Tom:

"Name's Mark Finn," begun I. "Most of you don't know about me without you've been to the farm I live on out in the country. I'm homeschooled there. I's born at the bottom of Arkansaw. Coming up, I spent a considerable stretch working the family farm. At the age of about eleven, I hooked up with a circus for a while; became an elephant handler, of all things. Next, I spent a summer on a whaler, which anchored time to time at the Port of New Orleans but traveled much of the globe. Warn't but two months at sea working on that whaler when the pirates struck. Nowadays folks don't hear much about pirates, but they're still out there. These pirates came for us off the coast of Somalia and they came fast.

Our captain knew how to outrun 'em and outmaneuver 'em, and he shook 'em. But lo and behold, in our haste, we run smack dab into the pirates' mothership. Facing certain destruction, we surrendered and was brought to shore and held for ransom.

'In Somalia, I was made to work briefly for the master pirate. I did everything from shining his shoes to running gold to a local merchant in exchange for vats of rum and some rare, multi-colored jewels, the likes of which I'd never seen, 'fore or since. They's about to take me out to sea and put me to work for 'em—you know, hunting loot—except that I escaped in the dead of night and snuck into steerage on an ocean-going freighter, which I rode till a chance arose to slip off at the Panama Canal. From there, one way or another, be it by train or car, donkey or horse, I made my way back to Arkansaw. Upon arriving, I seen that my parents had left word that they'd set themselves up in Missoura. I found 'em, and now I'm here."

Upon finishing my tale, I looked out to the judges in the front row and saw wide eyes. I glanced over at Mrs. Hawkins. She hadn't commented during the Tom and Becky presentations up to then. But she leaned into her podium microphone now and said, "Wow, that must've been quite an ordeal." Then she picked up off the podium her little notebook and went to grab her pen, seemingly to jot down some notes. She fumbled to locate her pen for a few moments; couldn't find it.

"This brings me," continued I, "to why I think I'd make a good Tom Sawyer. One thing Tom did impeccably well was tell stretchers. He whaled bigger than anyone in the whole county and probably beyond. I can whale, too. In fact, the story I just told you about the pirates and Somolia ain't true." Randy and some of the other kids in the crowd smiled at that.

"Tom could borrow on the sly, as well," continued I, glancing toward the podium and Mrs. Hawkins. I removed the microphone I was speaking into from its stand and walked toward her. "He could take a ladle right out from under Aunt Polly's nose and then, after watching Aunt Polly search the kitchen for it high and low, return the ladle to plain sight without her realizing, like magic," said I, pulling a pen out of my pocket and holding it up for all to see.

"Here's your pen, Mrs. Hawkins," continued I, handing it to her. The crowd cheered and she smiled. She grabbed for the pen, only, jest before handing it to her, I pulled it back and said, "Now, this here pen isn't actually yours. It's Mr. Testa's." I looked at Mr. Testa. He patted his shirt pocket to check. "Your pen, Mrs. Hawkins, is back on the podium right where you left it. I managed to sneak it back, jest like Tom would Aunt Polly's ladle."

Mrs. Hawkins looked down at the podium and let out a small gasp when she saw the pen. She picked it up for all to see, shaking her head and smiling. The Toms and Beckys out in the crowd cheered some more. I gave a quick bow and stepped off the stage. On my way back to my seat, I gave Mr. Testa his pen back. At my seat, Randy nudged me and said, "Mark, that was goated." I didn't know exactly what he was saying, but his body language told me he thought I'd done a good job.

———

Once all the Toms finished, Randy and I walked out to the lobby. He led me over to a gaggle of girls of which Lucy was a part. Several had their phones out, naturally, and they was all talking excitedly.

"We're getting ice cream," one of 'em says to Randy. "Want to join us?"

"Sure," says he, pulling me along.

Next I knows, I'm strolling the sidewalk alongside Lucy Thoreau.

"That was pretty clever, Mark," Lucy says.

"Thank you," says I. "Didn't really come up with it till the last second. Actually, I think the way you played matters got me to thinking about it a little differently."

"Well, it worked," said Lucy. "I bet you make it among the final twelve Toms."

"Reckon you'll make the Beckys," says I.

Lucy smiled. "Thank you. We'll see."

She paused a few moments before saying, "You know, Mark, when I first met you I mentioned that you say things in an interesting way, differently than most. You use words that I don't come across much except in old books, words like reckon. I like it."

"Well, I reckon I'll keep at it then."

At the shop, we ordered ice cream and ate outside amongst picnic tables.

"Marvelous job today, ladies," Randy said to the group.

"Thank you," Jessica said.

"I don't know," said Lucy. "The judges were kind of hard to read...didn't you all think so? I mean, Mrs. Brown is like a poker face. I can never tell what she's thinking."

"Agreed," said Randy. "But, come on, who's not on Team Lucy?"

Jessica nodded toward another group of kids jest a short ways off.

"Charlotte," Randy said quietly, chuckling. "Yes, I suppose she's not Team Lucy."

"You two stop it," said Lucy. "I have no problem with her."

"She has a problem with you," says Randy, "because you're genuine and not two-faced and people like you."

"Oh my gosh, you need to stop it," says Lucy.

"Mr. Smullens didn't seem too pleased with your magic trick act," Jimmy said. He was another one of Randy's friends.

"What a bore that guy," Randy added. Lucy giggled and nodded.

"I caught Mrs. Klein nodding off a time or two during a few of the Toms," Jimmy said. He pulled out his phone and showed us a picture he'd taken on the sly of her dozing.

"You took a picture?" a girl asked.

"Oh, my," said Jessica.

"It was kind of funny," Jimmy said, shrugging.

"She was probably bored because she already knows the few contestants she'd so much as consider voting for," said Randy.

"Yeah, like three or four country club boys," Jimmy said.

"Rumor has it," Lucy chimed in, "that she and Mr. Smullens are organizing a trip for this year's Tom and Becky to go to China, Shanghai."

"Makes sense. Apparently the Smullens family are like joint partners in factories there," said Randy. "My sister tells me he talks about it in his econ class."

Charlotte and her group paused as they were walking by us. "I see you have some new friends," says Charlotte to Lucy. Lucy looked puzzled by the comment. Charlotte had said it in an odd tone, too, and hadn't so much as looked at Randy or I. "Some of the girls," continued Charlotte, "are having a little get together at Parker-Wallace's. Maybe you and your friends want to come?"

"Maybe," said Lucy.

"Let's go, girls," said Charlotte, glancing behind her. "Cheerio," she added in passing, rather smugly.

"My goodness," said Lucy to no one in particular.

"Classic move. Host a get-together after the Tom and Becky speeches. I'm sure Charlotte's parents will be at the Wallace's. And judges Klein and Smullens, other hobnobbers." Randy leaned toward me, "Have you seen *Game of Thrones?*"

"No."

"You're in it."

CHAPTER TEN

Later the next week, I found myself at Orion's, charting stars, then working on features of his latest Rube Goldberg Machine, namely, right-sizing a balloon and rigging a mini, guillotine-like chopper. Orion designed it so that the chopper would pop the balloon, creating a burst of air which would nudge a small ball off a ledge leading to the machine's next element. After several run-throughs, Orion deemed himself satisfied. So we went upstairs--me to his office to work on the Tom and Becky essay, Orion out to the deck to gaze at the stars.

The essay called on us to explain why Tom and Becky mattered, and in turn why the Tom and Becky contest did. I'd put thought into it the previous few nights, as I lay awake at Pap's.

Sure, Tom had his flaws, wrote I now: he whaled, he stole, he showed out, he played hooky. But there was an original element to Tom that jest can't be denied. His imagination, his yarn-spinning, knew no bounds. His ability to draw people into his wild, largely make-believe adventures, knew no rival. I wrote out examples. Wrapping up matters, I determined that if Tom's capacity for adventure and conjuring, his uncommon persuasiveness and unrivaled energy, and his general optimism didn't capture something of the American essence then I ain't Mark Finn. Of course I ain't—but you know what I mean.

As for the importance of the Tom and Becky contest, I tied it back to keeping that spirit of imagination and inventiveness alive, and I wove in some of the ideas Lucy put forth in her Becky speech about independence of mind.

I printed the essay and was fitting to push on, when Orion, having peeled away from his telescope and set down his notepad, asked if I wanted a Moon Pie.

"Sure," says I.

We went down to the kitchen, where he rummaged through a cabinet. We took a seat at the kitchen island.

I spotted an old picture on the refrigerator, of Orion as a young man, alongside a beautiful young woman. They were holding shoes up to the camera, smiling big and carefree.

"Who's she?" asks I.

"My late wife, Ruthanne. Married fifty-eight years, the love of my life."

"Where are you all in this picture?"

"Right here, St. Petersburg, at a local shoe factory which her family partly owned. Into the 1960s St. Petersburg ranked among the nation's leaders in shoemaking. Her family even had its own shoe line. We'd been dating for less than a year. Married soon after."

"It's a mighty fine picture," says I.

"Yes," said Orion. "She passed away three years ago. That's why I took up volunteering at the museum. Needed to get out, stay active."

I nodded. Thought about how in a way that's why I first went to the museum, too.

"What happened to the factory?" asked I.

"Ah, now that's a long story. By the time of the sale, seeing as Ruthanne and I were married, I was a partial owner as well. But we were young and pursuing our careers and didn't have much say in the matter. Short version is that the Smullens family convinced a majority of the owners to merge with a production firm rooted in Asia."

"You mean the family of the Tom and Becky judge Smullens?"

"That's right. I suppose the operation was going to have to go somewhere, the way things looked. But Ruthanne and I regretted the whole thing later."

"Why's that?"

"Well, soon after operations moved to China a 'new' factory out there popped up right next to ours, employing our technology. In time, but not till after we'd drained a lot of resources, our company was put out of business. The Smullenses and a couple of their allies were the only ones still involved by then. They got a payout, enough to set up trusts to draw on. And they'd been invited, we found out later, to invest in the 'new' plant. I guess if you can't beat 'em, join 'em. As for St. Petersburg, pretty much all the factories shut down."

"And is this your daughter?" asked I, pointing to another picture.

"Yes. She lives in Germany now. She's a scientist, too, an astronomer. Studying abroad, she met a fellow from Germany, an engineer, and they eventually settled there. They have two daughters."

"She looks like her mom."

"How 'bout your family?" asks Orion.

Had to consider them three brothers and three sisters I'd conjured for Lucy. "As I say, my parents is a li'l peculiar. They keep to themselves. So we don't see a whole lotta other family," said I, being vague. "And they're all grown up; all three brothers, three sisters."

"Wow," says Orion. "Do you see them much?"

"No, they're all sorta scattered."

"Any other family around, aunts and uncles, cousins?" asks Orion.

"Oh, some down in the bottom of Arkansaw. We visit time to time."

"Mmm," says Orion, sort of gazing off, like he was thinking. "How do you like the Moon Pie?"

"Mighty good."

He slapped the counter and stood, before asking, "When's this essay on Tom due?"

"Tomorrow," says I as we walked to the front door. "I need to drop it off at the B&B Theater. By week's end, they'll have judged the essays and posted the final twenty-four contestants."

He nodded.

"You know what time they post the finalists?" asked I.

"Friday afternoon, I believe," says Orion. "Not long after school's out."

"See you then if not before," says I, heading out and pedaling away, first to the B&B Theater to slide my essay through the mail slit, then off to Pap's.

On Friday, I fished out the Spacelander and started for town. A stream of hopeful Toms and Beckys was converging on the museum as I rolled up. I spotted Randy.

"Good to see you, Mark," says he. "Look at your bike… looks like something out of *Star Trek*."

I smiled. "How are you?"

"I'm a little nervous. Usually there's a lot of talk at school about who made it. Not much chatter this year. I mean, there are the shoo-ins, of course: Parker-Wallace, Sterling, Charlotte, Lucy. But little else. I don't know what's up."

A group had already formed outside the museum's front window, onto which they would post the list of finalists. Excited chatter rose up as a worker, with a sheet of paper in hand, appeared from inside the museum and approached the front window. As he posted the list, kids craned their necks, searching for their names. Some walked away faces bright, others looking glum. Randy and I made our way through the gaggle and leaned toward the window. On the Becky side of the list, I spotted Lucy's name straight away. And at first glance to the Tom side, I saw Parker-Wallace's name. My heart sunk a bit, but then I heard Randy say, "We made it," jest as my eyes fell on my name and a moment later Randy's.

"We did," says I.

"What do you know?" asks he. "We made it." He stood in a sort of daze for several moments.

When he came to, we headed for the ice cream parlor. I could tell Randy's wheels were spinning. Finally, he said, "I mean, you in particular pulled a big upset, Mark. Just weeks ago, you were an unknown. You did a heckuva job. A heckuva job. Tom speech, fantastic. And your essay must've been a hit. Gotta hand it to you, Mark. Big upset."

"Thank you," says I.

Randy looked me over, stopping his gaze on my moccasins for a few moments.

"I'm not sure you even know how big of an upset you just pulled," added he. "I mean, you wear baggy football jerseys of teams nobody's heard of; you cut your pants off at the calf; you don't cut your hair. And, as I say, you're essentially unheard of. I've asked around. Nobody knows who you are. And, no offense, you wear moccasins.

Sometimes you go barefoot. You have the most bizarre, yet beautiful, bicycle I've ever seen. Then there's this sense that you have a real grasp for Tom and Huck, like you truly get them. This whole scenario is actually giving me hope. I gotta give credit to the judges who have given you a shot. This is a welcome surprise."

He paused a few moments before continuing, "Perhaps, it's that you're such a delightful enigma that a few of the judges decided what the heck, let's roll the dice—it's harmless, kind of fun. But maybe they actually see it, too."

"See what?" asks I.

"You have it," says Randy.

"Have what?" asks I.

"Authenticity," says Randy. "You're the real deal, Mark Finn."

"Well, I appreciate that Randy. I think you're authentic enough to fake it that you're Tom, too." He smiled. "I'm glad we both made it. Congratulations to you," added I.

Randy went to thinking for a few moments. "It gets tougher from here," said he. "There's a formal dinner in a couple of weeks. We get judged at it. They don't explicitly tell us that we get judged at it. But believe me, we get judged at it."

I nodded.

"Lotta moving parts, Mark. We need to strategize."

"Okay," says I.

"Let's meet at my house, Thursday afternoon?"

"Sounds all right by me."

"My older sister, she's kinda bossy, but she'll want to help us. And she can. I have a younger brother, too, just so you know. It's them and me and my mom."

"Sounds good," says I.

Outside the ice cream shop, I slid the Spacelander into the bike rack. Inside, I spotted Lucy. Parker-Wallace and Sterling and a couple of other boys in their gang were milling about, too, having already gotten their ice cream. A few of 'em looked over toward Randy and I as we stepped in, whispered amongst each other, and then smirked and shook their heads.

"We're not their favorites," says Randy.

"They're not ours," says I.

Took a minute, but we made it to the front. Randy ordered. The cashier looked at me, "What would you like?"

I'd looked at the prices. "Nuthing for me," says I. "But thank you."

"You're not getting anything?" asks Randy.

"Nah," says I, leaning in toward him so as not to be overheard. "I can get a bucket of ice cream at the store for the same as that cone."

"You've got a point," says he.

Upon receiving his ice cream, he led me over to a group of kids, Lucy among 'em. Parker-Wallace's crew was alongside.

"Congratulations," a boy named Robbie says to Randy.

"You too," says Randy.

"What's your name again?" Robbie asks, looking at me.

"Mark," says I.

"Did you get picked?" asks he.

"Yes, I did," says I, stealing a glance toward Lucy. She smiled a little.

"Well, congratu…" started Robbie before one of the boys in Parker-Wallace's group, a kid named Houston, cut in.

"Yeah, the homeschooled kid who goes barefoot got picked while others more deserving got sent home," says he. Parker-Wallace and the rest of their cronies smirked our way.

"Give it a rest. You're just sore because not all your friends got picked," says Randy.

"The pretty boy says to be quiet," threw in Parker-Wallace, eliciting snide chuckles.

I saw Randy freeze a bit at that. His face turned red.

"Why don't you go hang out with the girls, pretty boy," says Houston, stepping toward Randy.

Quick as a whip, I slid in front of Houston.

"I think we're good here," says I, nearly face to face now. I'd learned this move from my Musketeer buddy, Tank, back in Rolling Dunes.

Houston stopped. I could see him thinking things through.

I warn't sure exactly how matters might unfold, but I knew I was in whole hog for a showdown right there if need be.

Parker-Wallace pulled Houston back. "Come on," says he. "Let's go. They're not worth it."

"Yeah, you're not worth it," says Houston.

Parker-Wallace, who was taller than me by a few inches, leaned toward my ear. "Some judges might think it cute to keep around the poor, little homeschooled kid," said he, in an intense whisper. "But I'm not buying your act. You're not gonna win and neither is your girlfriend."

He pulled away. "Nothing to see here," says he, loudly, to folks looking on.

He led his crew outside the parlor.

"Let's get out of here," says I to Randy.

"Yeah," says he.

Starting for the door, we heard Lucy say, "Hey, Randy, Mark…"

We turned back.

She stepped toward us. "I just wanted to say congratulations. I'm glad you both made it. I think it should be fun."

Randy nodded, still a little shaken up.

"Glad you made it, too, Lucy," says I.

I pulled the Spacelander off the bike rack. Randy hadn't said anything on the way out. But now he put his hand on my shoulder and said, "Thanks, Mark. Appreciate you stepping in."

"Oh, 'twas nuthing," says I.

"'Twas nuthing, uh?" says he, smiling a little.

"Yeah. An old friend, Tank, he learned me good," says I.

"Well, I'm glad he learned you good. And I'm glad we're friends."

"Me too," says I.

CHAPTER ELEVEN

I pedaled over to Orion's to let him know I'd made the final twelve Toms.

"Mark, welcome," says he, greeting me, notebook in hand. I could tell half his attention was on me and half on whatever he'd been working on. Suddenly, he sort of became fully present and waved me in, saying, "The competition. Congratulations. You made the cut. Moon Pies."

"Thank you," says I.

I sat at the island.

"You must really know your Tom," said he, with that twinkle in his eye.

"Reckon if I know anyone, I know that misbehaving, adventure-wheeling, rapscallion," said I.

"I'm happy for you. This afternoon I was at the museum. I had planned to come outside to say hello, you know, when they posted the list of finalists. But I found myself caught in the most peculiar meeting."

"That so?" asks I.

"Yes, up in Jack's office, the Museum's president," said Orion, his manner turning a bit more serious. "Jack asked me to join the meeting because I've made it a bit of a passion to study Tom and Huck. Well, there was this man, large man, at the meeting—he had a couple of suit-clad others with him—and he made a rather odd request."

I got nervous a-sudden, not sure where this was going. "Oh yeah?" wonders I.

"First, this man tells us that he has an original Huckleberry Finn pipe."

My eyes widened.

Orion continued. "The man says he has a few other things of Huck's, too, and that if we let him get DNA from some of our original artifacts to compare with his items, he can easily prove it."

I went cold a moment, "Seems ruther preposterous."

"That's what I thought. But this man was insistent. He showed us the pipe and he presented a copy of the DNA report he'd commissioned from it."

I had a vague notion of DNA from biology class in Rolling Dunes.

"What's this man's name?" asks I, expectantly.

"Dr. Knotts," says Orion.

I tried to show no emotion.

"This Dr. Knotts," continued Orion, "told us that there's even more to the story. But he didn't elaborate. He said, as a first step, he wanted Jack to agree to let him run the DNA tests."

"Is he going to let him?" asks I.

"Well, we were discussing it. Jack seemed a little hesitant. Then Dr. Knotts pulled out his checkbook and wrote in a big number. That settled the matter."

My mind started a-running. Need to keep calm, think things through, says I to myself.

Shifting gears, Orion stood up and said, "Well, what do you say we do some star-gazing?"

"Sure," says I, shakily.

I lay awake late that night a-turning matters over. Lighting out made some sense; only I didn't want to. Not now, leastways. I had a place to stay in Pap's cabin, and I wanted to see this Tom and Becky thing through. Dr. Knotts warn't likely to know my whereabouts, at least yet, judged I. And, truth is, Lucy steady come to mind. She was someone I needed to get to know, plain and simple. I felt it deep in my bones. Avoiding Dr. Knotts and his gang till they pushed on seemed doable. Still, shuteye played keepaway.

In the morning, I kept churning matters. Really, the next several days I did so. One evening I rode over to Orion's to help with his Goldberg machine, chart some stars, make a little cash, but mainly to fish for an update on Dr. Knotts. Orion told me the museum had given him an artifact to take back with him and have tested. Dr. Knotts planned to return in a week or so with results.

———

On Thursday that week, as planned, I went to Randy's. He lived in a ruther regular home, for nowadays, near to town.

As we stepped into the kitchen, Randy's mom greeted us with a smile.

"Mom, this is Mark. Mark, this is my mom."

"Hello, Mark. I'm Sheila. Welcome."

"Yes'm," says I.

"Did you all have a nice day at school?"

"Mark's homeschooled."

"Oh, yes, that's right," says she. "Would you boys like a snack?"

"Yes, please," says Randy.

"Great, I'll make some sandwiches."

Randy grabbed a chair at a table jest off the kitchen, and I joined him.

By and by his sister come down from upstairs. Randy introduced us. She sized me a few moments and looked back to Randy. "Are you two going to prepare to be Tom this afternoon?"

"Yea," says Randy.

She glanced back at me. "We are going to need to work on your hair."

I smiled a little.

"Sharon," says Randy's mom, shaking her head.

"Tell him how you think," says Randy.

"Yours, too," says she, eyeing Randy. She sat down at the table and looked at me. "Do you have an outfit?"

"How do you mean?" asks I.

"For the dinner."

"Well, I mean, I probably…"

"Probably?" says she. "You need an outfit. This dinner is a big deal. I know they say it's not an official part of the competition. But believe me, it is part of the competition." She looked at Randy. "We need to go shopping."

"I'm up for shopping," says Randy.

"Hair and shopping, fabulous," says Sharon. "Let's go to the Huck."

Wait, thinks I, did she just call me Huck?

"Huck?" asked I.

"Yea, the Huck Finn shopping center."

"Oh, the Huck."

"Do you not get out much?" asked she with a friendly smirk. "We'll start with J.C. Penney's."

At J.C. Penney's, Randy and Sharon looked through racks of clothes, picking out outfits, sport coats and slacks, setting aside accessories, ties, belts, Sunday shoes. Randy found a few combinations he liked. Tried a couple on. Sharon approved of one. They handed me several items next and directed me to try them on. Several times they had me change into an outfit and step out into the general area so they could assess the 'fit,' tug on my shirt, straighten my jacket.

"This is too long…That's too short," they'd say. "Oh I like that…Tuck this in."

Finally, Sharon stood me in front of a mirror and nodded.

"Yes, that's it," says Randy, as all three of us stared back at me. "That's the look."

They had me bound up in a ruther tight-fitting dark suit, my waist wrapped by a belt, my neck lassoed by a tie.

"I don't know," says I, suddenly nervous about the whole thing.

"It's great," says Randy. "I know it's outside of your comfort zone, but this is it."

"Seems ruther smothery."

"Beauty has a price," says Sharon.

"Listen, Mark, we gotta go for it. I mean, you don't want Parker-Wallace and his crew as the only Toms standing there in the finals with Lucy and the rest of the girls, do you?"

I didn't want that.

"Boys, we gotta keep moving," says Sharon. "We need to work on your hair, both of yours."

On our way to checkout, Sharon quick-grabbed a polyester, Fedora-style hat which had been made to look like a straw hat. She grabbed suspenders, too, then looked at me and said, "Later in the competition, you're going to need a Tom Sawyer outfit. This'll do." At the register, a lady rung us up. I peeled back bills to pay for my portion.

Sharon stopped us next at Dollar General for hair product. While she browsed, Randy and I ended up in the games section. Randy found a magic kit, held it up, and said, "Great for dinner parties. I wish I knew magic." He set down the kit and held up a deck of cards. "Card tricks, too. It'd be nice to know a few."

"I know a couple," says I, thinking of time I'd spent on riverboats observing the sharps.

"Really?"

"Nothing too fancy. But yeah."

Randy pulled out the cards. "Show me a trick."

"Okay," says I.

I found an ace and two lower cards, showed the three cards to Randy, then placed 'em facedown on the ground and said, "Let's see if you can track the ace."

"I got this," says Randy, kneeling down in front of the cards.

I moved the cards slowly at first, over and across each other, so they'd exchange places. Once or twice, I flipped up the ace to build Randy's confidence in its whereabouts. Picking up the pace, I kept the cards a-moving, flashing the ace another time, till *Whoosh!* I pulled the monte. With three cards now facedown on the ground in a row, I slid 'em from spot to spot a final time and asked, "Where's the ace?"

"Right here," Randy says with confidence, putting his finger on top of one of the cards.

I turned it face-up.

"What!?" says he.

I flipped over the card next to his choice and said, "It's this one."

"How'd you do that? Do it again."

This time I did the "double monte," a move I learned late one night on the Mighty from an old, legendary sharp. When it comes to dealing the double, the trick is to—jest as the two cards you would usually "monte" are crossing—use your off-hand to subtly slide the third card across and under so as to land in the middle of the three. It's a risky but deadly move. I managed it, and sure enough, Randy guessed the wrong card again.

"What!?" said he again. He put his finger on one of the two remaining face-down cards. "It's there, then."

"Nope," says I, turning it over.

His eyes widened further. "Get outta here."

I explained the move.

"The 'double monte,'" says he. "I like it."

"Hey numbskulls?"

Randy and I looked up from the cards and saw Sharon staring down at us.

"We gotta go."

Back at Randy's, Sharon went to work on his hair first. She sprayed awful smelling product on his hair and rubbed foam in it and tussled it, and time to time spritzed water on it. "Teasing it," said she. Finally, she stepped back and studied her work. Satisfied, she handed Randy a mirror. He seemed pleased with the outcome.

As I say, my hair had gotten rather long and full and unruly and somehow curlier than usual. She pulled out the pungent spray, then the foam, and went to shaping and teasing. "A lot to tame," she said a time or two. My hair tingled and itched. Couple times, she looked over to Randy, and he threw in his hay on how it looked. Finally, they declared themselves satisfied. "But you're going to need a haircut. Nothing too drastic; a trim for sure."

Sharon instructed us to go change into our new out-fits. "When you're done, we'll meet in the dining room," she explained. "We have dinner table etiquette to go over." She sounded like Miss Watson.

Back downstairs in my smothery garb I grabbed a seat at the dining table. Randy's brother Mikey sat along-side me. Multiple plates sat in front of each chair. At the center of the table were several napkins and double the amount of silverware you'd expect for a dinner this size. Sharon came in from the kitchen with more ware.

"Ready soon," Randy's mom said from the kitchen.

While we waited, Randy grabbed a deck of cards from a nearby bureau and said, "Mark, how about you show Mikey that card trick?"

I picked out three cards and explained to Mikey that he needed to track the ace. He watched closely as I moved the cards. When it came time, he seemed quite confident. But sure was surprised when I flipped his choice over. He asked me to do the trick again jest as Sharon strode back in.

"No, no, no," said she, shaking her head. "No time for silliness. Grab a seat. Grab a seat."

She started in on a few rules for a formal dinner. When Mikey realized what was happening, he said there remained plenty of time in his life to learn fine dining mumbo-jumbo, but this evening was not one of those times. He scooted out from his seat, declaring, "I'm going upstairs to hit the sticks."

At Sharon's direction, Randy and I each grabbed two spoons, two knives, and two forks and placed 'em on the side of our plates. Above each plate, one of which was big, the other small, we added another spoon and fork—no whaling. Sharon had us put napkins atop each big plate, too. *Now, why napkins where the food should go?* wondered I. Randy's mom, toting a salad bowl, joined us. She and Sharon proceeded to go over more rules of etiquette, many of them ruther bizarre and awful particular.

"I don't see how someone's supposed to remember all this," declared Randy.

"Where's Mikey?" asked Sheila. Sharon explained. Sheila rolled her eyes and called Mikey down before she and Sharon went back into the kitchen.

Mikey shuffled to his seat. Soon after, Sheila and Sharon stepped back in with a tray of soups. Randy and I were eager to dig in. But Randy's mom stopped short of the table and looked at us like we'd done something wrong. We sorta shrugged, unsure as to what she was getting at. She nodded toward Sharon's chair. 'Stead of sitting down, Sharon stood alongside it. Randy and I looked at each other again. Then it seemed to dawn on him, because he quickly popped up and pulled his sister's chair out for her. Hopping up as well, I waited for Randy's mom to serve the soup and then pulled her chair out for her.

Seated, Sharon asked us to rehash the utensil etiquette we'd learned: this particular fork at this time, a different fork for another time. Soup spoon now, regular spoon later. With that covered, we ate in silence for a bit, till Sharon said, "Now, we need to talk about dinner conversation." She leaned forward. "Here's the deal: be pleasant and interesting but stay away from politics and religion. Ask about your fellow guests' lives, what their families are like, what they do, where they're from. And don't forget to compliment the chef. The host, as well, if they are not one and the same."

Randy's mom threw in her shovel. "You don't know which judge, or judge's confidant, will be seated at your table, observing you. Nor which fellow contestants you might be seated with. So you should come with conversation ideas in mind; maybe ask what someone's favorite book or movie is."

"Yeah, like if you're seated with Mr. Testa, ask him why he shows so much chest hair," Randy said, chuckling.

"Randy," scolded his mom, though I could tell she was slightly amused. She offered, "Maybe you could ask him and Mr. Smullens how local businesses are doing. They have business interests, and Mr. Smullens teaches economics."

"Don't ask him about sunk cost," Sharon butted in. "He tried to explain it the other day in class. Made no sense. He said if you buy a Honda for like $20,000 it may lose, let's say, ten percent of its value when you drive it off the lot. But you'd still be up $18,000 because the twenty was sunk. I mean, what the 'ell?"

"Sharon, that is not formal dinner language," said her mom. "And I doubt that's exactly how sunk cost was presented."

"It was. I was there. Sunk forty minutes listening."

Randy's mom sighed as she got up from the table. "Randy and Mark, can you please clear the soup bowls?"

We rose.

Soon, she brung in the main course.

"Do you boys remember which fork we use next?" asks Randy's sister.

I looked at my plate, trying to recall. Could be the one atop the plate or the one to the left of it, which I also hadn't yet used.

"The one to your left, on the inside," says Randy.

"Correct," says Sharon.

"I'm a little afraid to ask given your characterizations of Testa and Smullens," said Randy's mom, "who are some of the other judges this year?"

"There's Mrs. Brown," says Randy.

"Love her," says Sharon. "Best teacher I ever had."

"Everyone loves her," said Randy's mom. "Both of you kids, all my friends' kids. A conversation starter for her could be to ask how she connects so well with elementary age students."

"I'm having a hard time envisioning myself asking that," said Randy. His mom rolled her eyes.

"There's Mrs. Klein. She's quite stuffy. Hoping I don't sit by her," said Randy.

"Okay, well, she's not my favorite either," admitted Randy's mom.

"Very hoity-toity. I don't get it. This isn't Martha's Vineyard. C'mon," says Sharon. "Sure, she's connected with St. Petersburg movers and shakers, like Parker-Wallace's family, Sterling Lewis's. And, yes, the boys need to bring their 'A' game no matter who you're sitting with. But, I mean, just don't act like you're better than everyone else. Plus her daughter is a mess."

"I'm not sure that's relevant," says Sheila.

"Okay, still, don't act like you're better than everyone," says Sharon.

"I'm sure," says Randy's mom, glancing at Randy and I, "that Mrs. Klein has some nice qualities. She's involved in the women's club, from what I understand. Loves bridge. Yes, she likes finer things…"

"She's a snob. Let's just admit it. I don't want to sit by her," said Randy.

Sheila looked at me. "My children are opinionated."

"I don't mind it, ma'am. I ruther enjoy it."

She looked at Randy. "Regardless of her tastes, she is a judge. And finding ways to connect with different sorts of people is a good skill to work on. It will serve you well in life, not just in the competition."

"Okay, so I should talk about how to be a great teacher with Mrs. Brown; talk chest hair, gold chains, motorcycles with Mr. Testa; Nantucket, the country club, and designer purses with Mrs. Klein; the restaurant business with Mrs. Hawkins; and cheap stuff from China with Mr. "Sunk Cost" Smullens?" asks Randy.

"You're a nut," says his mom.

CHAPTER TWELVE

Later the next week, after charting stars, I asked Orion how things were going at the museum, hoping he'd offer an update on the DNA tests Dr. Knotts undertook, yet not wanting to seem like I was prying. He said things was fine, nothing out of the ordinary. For a few moments he went to thought, then asked, "You mean anything new with the Dr. Knotts fella?"

"Yeah," says I.

"Funny you should ask," says Orion. "We got word today that, at least according to him, the DNA is a match. So, somehow, I guess he has Huck Finn's old pipe—and a few other items which used to be Huck's. I've been doing a little research on this Dr. Knotts. I know some people in the industry that he's, shall we say, dabbled in. Peculiar guy."

"That so?" feigned I. He nodded, then added, "Anyway, the whole thing has caused quite a stir amongst our board."

Now that Dr. Knotts had his DNA match, he'd really want to find me, reckoned I, parade me about and put me on some sort of money-grabbing tour, turn me into a kind of living attraction, like a traveling zoo creature. That warn't how I wanted to live.

"What do you think he's going to do next?" asked I.

"I don't know?" says Orion. He looked at me reassuringly. "But I'm keeping tabs."

I nodded.

"Let's look at some constellations," said Orion. "I have you hunting obscure stars, but I don't think I've shown you the best-known constellations."

He had me look through the main telescope.

"Do you see the ladle shape?" asked he.

"Um, uh, I think so," said I. He was patient.

"You find it?"

"Don't think so," says I.

He proceeded to describe from heart my field of vision, as if he was looking through the 'scope his ownself. Finally, I spotted it. Next, he directed me toward Pegasus. He guided me to look thisaway, then thataway, to connect this star with that star. But I warn't making heads or tails of it.

"You see it?" asked he.

"I don't think so," admitted I.

"Wait, wait a minute," says Orion excitedly. "Should have thought of this sooner. My daughter had me download an app which enables my tablet to communicate with the telescopes."

He rushed into his office and returned soon after, tablet in-hand. He turned it on and tapped the screen a few times.

"Ah, yes," says he, holding up the tablet. "Look there. The tablet screen shows the telescope's view of the sky. All right, I just need to put the tablet in illustrator mode. Mark, now look back under the telescope. Do you see the Pegasus now?" He'd outlined it, connecting star to star.

"Will you look at that?" says I. "Yes, I sure do."

"Pegasus sprung from Medusa's blood," explained he. "Like a phantom, timeless."

He was peering upward as if in awe. Then he looked at me. Couldn't help but wonder if he was trying to tell me something.

———

Afternoon the next day, I pedaled to Randy's to meet before the formal dinner. His sister Sharon sat me in a chair and told me she must trim my hair. I let her. She sprayed it and fussed with it, too. I tried squashing that but she warn't to be denied. She had her mom come in to help assess as well. They revisited their instructions for how Randy and I was to comport ourselves at the dinner, too. When they were satisfied, Randy and I clumb into Sharon's car, and she drove us to Rockcliffe Mansion.

We rolled onto the mansion's sweeping driveway, curving around tree-laden grounds, till we come to a stop under the porte-cochere.

"Love me some old Victorian homes," says Sharon.

"And porte-cocheres. Big fan," says Randy.

Sharon turned to look back at us. "Alright, young men. Formal dinner time. Good luck."

"Thank you," says Randy.

"Yes, thank you, ma'am," says I.

Greeters led us into the Rockcliffe, pointing out the great room in which we were to eat and in which a banjo picker and guitar strummer were playing music. Meantime, folks milled about various rooms of the house. As Randy and I strolled through the place, our eyes bulged on account of the Rockcliffe having all the stuffings of a Thanksgiving turkey: gilded chandeliers, pink marble, intricately carved wood paneling, fireplaces. Fine furniture all around. Soon, Randy and I came upon what they called the music room. It featured grand pianos in opposite corners. Two grand pianos in one room. Lucy and a couple others hoping to be Becky were inside talking. Randy nudged me in.

"Hello, girls," says Randy in his easy and carefree way. "You all look wonderful this evening."

"Why, thank you, Randy," says Lucy, sort of curtsying. "You two clean up nicely."

I felt myself blush.

Charlotte stepped over. She made a show of greeting Randy with a big hug. This made it so we all had to hug or else it'd be kind of awkward. When my turn come to give Lucy a hug, my heart galloped.

"Good to see you," says Lucy.

I cleared my throat. "You look nice as pie," says I.

The girls giggled at that. Lucy blushed a bit. "Thank you," said she.

There was a brief, awkward silence amongst us before Randy put his hands out, glanced around the room, and asked, "How about this place?"

"It's amazing," says Veronica.

"Yes, remarkable," says Charlotte, a little affected-like.

"I mean the Tiffany glass touch," said Randy, glancing at the chandelier.

I took a quick look around, at the bronze statues on the mantle, the ornately carved wood trim, the wallpaper featuring gold-dusted flowers, and the Tiffany glass Randy had pointed out. "Ruther understated," said I. Lucy chuckled at that.

Right then a call to dinner bellowed forth. Everybody started shuffling toward the great room. But before fully exiting the music room, Randy nudged me to hold back a moment. He nodded ahead toward Lucy. "I think she might like you."

I was hopeful, but being unschooled and generally low-down and unmannered, gave me pause. "You do?" asked I.

He nodded and shrugged, as if to say, *I think so.*

'Bout then, Parker-Wallace and Sterling and another of their crew made it to the bottom of the Rockcliffe's double staircase, and there our paths crossed.

"What do we have here?" Parker-Wallace condescended as they got close. His buddies laughed.

"What do we have here?" asked Randy, sarcastically.

Speaking low as he passed us, Parker-Wallace said, "Losers, for one."

"Yeah," says Sterling.

"Very original," says Randy.

"You know what your problem is, Randy?" asks Parker-Wallace, still talking low. "You think you're so smart. But you're not. If you were so smart, why would you be hanging with him?" He nodded my way. "I'm not buying his act. He's a phony. And so are you."

———

In the great room, we were instructed to find our nameplates at one of the four meticulously set tables, each of which sat ten people. As Randy and I worked our way further into the room, I noticed Lucy looking in my direction. She seemed to be waving someone over to her. I looked behind me but saw no one in particular. Looking back at her, I saw her wave again. *She's waving at us*, realized I. Randy and I made our way to her. Sure enough, our assigned seats, with nameplate and all, were at her table. Jest one seat separated Lucy and me.

Soon thereafter, Parker-Wallace approaches our table and pulls out a chair, across from mine. He looked at Lucy and said hello and did the same for Stacey, a Becky also at our table. He didn't so much as glance at me or Randy. Of a sudden, he popped quickly out of his chair and pulled out the one next to him for another contestant who'd stepped up, Jessica.

"Isn't that sweet," said the finely dressed "Nantucket" judge, Mrs. Klein, as she stepped to our table. Parker-Wallace pulled out her chair, too.

"What a gentleman," says she.

A boy named Alvin sat at our table. And up steps Mr. "Sunk Cost" Smullens, the economist. He sat down directly to my right. I looked to Randy. On the sly, he shrugged slightly. These warn't the judges we'd hoped to sit with. A fella by the name of JJ Sloan, a local business-man, jewelry store owner, rounded out our table. He sat in the spot between Lucy and me. I remembered to take the napkin off my plate and put it on my lap. Randy did the same. His mom would've been pleased.

A lady of the family who owns the Rockcliffe stepped to a microphone set up in front of the great room's fireplace. She welcomed us, thanked the Chamber of Commerce and other contest sponsors, and congratu-lated us contestants on making it this far and praised our outfits. She introduced the judges and asked them to say a few words. Mrs. Klein walked up first. She reminded us that, were we to win Tom or Becky, we'd be asked to din-ners like this routinely. She urged us to use this one as a chance to gain experience. She finished by declaring it a considerable societal honor to be named Tom or Becky.

I was distracted when the next judge, Mrs. Brown, came up to offer words, because I realized how powerful hungry I was. Between the uncertainty of the contest and getting ready at Randy's, I hadn't eaten much all day.

Judge Smullens spoke next. He talked about the importance of Tom and Becky, Huck and Jim, the whole shebang, to St. Petersburg's economy. He gave us a quick history of the room we were in and of the Rockcliffe Mansion itself. While he talked, I kept a-eyeing the little dish of what looked like vanilla ice cream out in front of my main plate. Now, this didn't look like regular vanilla ice cream, mind you. It appeared super-fancy, had qualities that made it seem extra fine: thick enough to keep its shape yet soft enough to sort of float on the dish. It had a fluffy, chevron pattern etched into it, too. My mouth watered as my eyes wandered to it.

Vaguely, I heard Mr. Smullens droning on about a marble-top table at the Rockcliffe which came from China, a teakwood piece from India, and a Persian rug. He loved stuff made elsewheres, thunk me, eyeing that ice cream.

Sort of mindlessly, and seeing as folks was focused on Mr. Smullens, I grabbed the spoon atop my plate and dipped it into the velvety cream. Quick-scooped a spoonful and brought it to my mouth, closing my eyes. Upon tasting it, however, I realized straight away that this warn't ice cream at all. 'Twas butter. Butter presented in the most appealing, ice cream-looking fashion you can imagine. Now you might think I'd've questioned the idea of them serving ice cream this early into dinner, but I hadn't. My first reflex was to spit it out. I mean, this was a lot of butter. 'Xcept I thought of how Sharon had warned us that we'd be watched and judged. Sure enough, when I opened my eyes, I saw Mrs. Klein staring at me with a horrified look on her face. I glanced to Lucy. She giggled a little and looked down at her plate. Randy couldn't hide a smile as he shook his head in disbelief. No one else seemed to notice. Mrs. Klein turned away. I just shrugged and, hungry as I was, decided to savor the butter best I could.

———

Dinner run along ruther uneventful thereafter: me minding my p's and q's, finding opportunities to connect with Lucy; Mrs. Klein acting quite proper, engaging in small talk; Mr. Smullens looking scholarly, making this point here, that point there. Near the end of the main course, the jeweler at our table, JJ Sloan, held up his gilded fork and looked at it. "Wonder what Tom would think of all this?" he sort of mused to his own self.

Others at the table was focused on their meal or having side conversations, but hearing Mr. Sloan wonder this about Tom and seeing him look again at that golden fork, got me to thinking of the gold the judge put out at interest for me and how plussed Tom got when the Judge had talked Aunt Polly into putting Tom's share of the loot out for interest, too. I leaned toward the jeweler and, without so much as thinking about it, said, "If Tom were here, he'd like to melt that fork down, trade it in, and spend the cash on some adventure."

The jeweler smiled. "What would you do with it?"

"I'd keep it out at interest, for now leastways," says I.

"There's nothing you'd want to buy?" asks Mr. Sloan.

I thought about it. "Not really," says I. "So long as I'm free to roam and fish and hunt and the like, I'd jest as well let that gold set there, wait till I really needed it. I have a little cash already for odds and ends noway."

"You know, it's interesting," said Mr. Sloan. "If you melted down all the gold that's ever been mined in all the history of the world, it wouldn't make but a cube that was about twenty meters high, twenty wide. That's it. In all the history of mankind."

"There you go," responded I. "As such, if you're lucky enough to get gold, putting it out at interest is the way. Till you really need it."

"That's foresight, young man," says the jeweler.

Our host returned to the mic to thank the chef and wait-staff for a fine dinner and to let us know that dessert would be coming along in about twenty minutes. Meantime, she encouraged us to tour the house and asked supporters of the Tom and Becky competition in attendance to consider the "limited but tastefully cho-sen" silent auction items on display in the parlor.

A group of us Toms and Beckys wound up back in the music room. We was jest sort of milling about, chatting, when a contestant, Stacey, sat at one of the grand pianos and begun playing a tune. Lucy sat next to her and started singing along, "Here comes the sun…" Another Becky joined in. They sounded sweeter than Carolina chickadees on a bright morn.

While the girls made music, a few of the boys opened some of the music room's cabinets. One cabinet had a bunch of games in it. Randy spotted a deck of cards inside, reached for it, and announced to the Toms, "Mark's got a trick. I'll bet any of you a dollar that he'll get you on it."

He placed the deck on a little round table near the center of the room and peeled several dollar bills out of his pocket.

Now, as I say, coming up, I spent time on the Muddy and learned tricks of the sharp. But I was thinking now maybe this warn't the time nor the place…'xcept then Parker-Wallace throws in his shovel, saying, "I'll bet a dollar."

"Me too," says Parker-Wallace's buddy, Sterling.

"I'll bet both of you," says Randy. Kids gathered around. Of a sudden, I got a little nervous.

I held up three cards, an ace among them, then put 'em facedown in a row.

"All you gotta do is track the ace. He'll move the cards, you track the ace," explained Randy. "You track the ace, you double your money."

Another boy threw a dollar in.

At first, I wove the cards slowly, showing one of 'em face up time to time. Going slow gives the observers confidence that they can track the ace. Steadily, I picked up the pace. Then, *whoosh!* Without so much as the slightest move, I pulled the monte.

I looked down at the three cards on the table. Randy asked, "Where's the ace?"

Parker-Wallace picked for hisself and Sterling. The third boy picked the same card. They picked wrong.

"Pay up, boys," says Randy, smiling.

"Do it again," says one of the girls in the back. "I didn't see it."

I warn't for doing it again 'cuz I've seen how emotions rise in these sort of situations.

"Nah, I don't think we need to…"

"That was lucky," says one of Parker's fellas.

"Yeah," says another. "He can't do it again."

"I'll bet double," says Parker.

"Me too," says Sterling.

I tried to give 'em an out by hesitating further, but they was all in, bills on the table. I started slow-weaving the cards again, letting the bettors' confidence build before speeding the cards up, showing one faceup here and there. Stakes was high, but I decided to risk the double monte. With the cards moving faster now, I focused in and then *Whoosh! Whoosh!* I did the monte with my right hand while sliding the third card middle with my other. The third slid jest under the one I'd sent a-flying. *It worked*, thunk I to myself.

Sterling slapped his hand down on the middle card. "I got it. That's it, that's the ace," says he.

"No, no, no," says Parker-Wallace as I turned up Sterling's choice.

"I knew it," says Parker-Wallace.

Randy, knowing I'd done the double, leaned in and said to Parker-Wallace, "Double it another time—jest between these two remaining cards, as they are."

"Sure," says Parker-Wallace. He tossed in more bills and smacked his hand on the card he wanted. I turned it over. The crowd gasped. It warn't the ace nuther.

"Call me money," said Randy, smiling, as he begun to sweep up the cash on the table.

Right then, Mrs. Hawkins and Mrs. Klein appeared at the music room's entryway, their eyes a-bulging. Mrs. Klein's breath seemed cut short. Looked like Mrs. Hawkins, though, had a hint of a smile she was trying to hide. All the kids naturally backed away. It was jest Randy and me at the table now, dollar bills and cards lying about. Mrs. Klein started to say something, but it came out more like a stammer. She composed herself and then managed, "Gambling? At the Tom and Becky formal dinner—and in the music room, no less?"

Mrs. Hawkins jumped in. "Boys and girls, dessert is being served. Please, back to the great room. Mark, Randy, put the cards away."

"Yes'm," says I.

As kids started filing out, Parker leaned in toward Randy and I and said under his breath, "You'll pay for this."

"I think you already did," says Randy, putting the money in his pocket. As we walked back to the great room, Randy nodded ahead toward Mrs. Klein. "I think it's fair to say she's not voting for either of us."

At dessert, the jeweler Sloan, asked about my upbringing. I spun about Arkansaw, of being homeschooled and living on a farm, the whole bit. He asked Lucy about her background, too.

Near dessert's end, Mr. Sloan leaned toward me and with a wry smile said quietly, "Heard there was a little choir practice in the music room?"

I warn't exactly sure what he meant. He must've sensed my confusion. Discreetly, he moved his hands to make as if he was dealing cards. He'd heard of our gambling surmised I. "Yes, sir," says I. "A little choir practice." He nodded.

Mrs. Hawkins stepped to the mic. "Hello everyone. If I can have your attention," said she. "Tonight, we are excited to announce a new wrinkle to this year's competition. Next week, our finalists will perform, in pairs at the B&B Theater, a scene from the *Adventures of Tom Sawyer.*

We have commissioned two background sets, one of MacDougal Cave, the other of Tom and Becky's schoolhouse. Each pair can choose a cave scene or schoolhouse scene. After these performances, we will narrow the field to eight contestants, four boys, four girls."

Mr. Sloan leaned toward Lucy and me, "You two should act out the scene together. You'd be great."

I looked at Lucy. She smiled, then looked down at her plate. *You gotta step up*, says I to myself, *Mr. Sloan jest cleared the deck for you.*

"I think that'd be awful nice," says I. Lucy looked at me. "What do you think?"

"Sure, yes, that sounds nice," says she.

"Well, then it's done," says Mr. Sloan.

———

The tables thinned as folks started making their way out of the Rockcliffe. I's planning to walk to Orion's but waited with Randy till his sister come to fetch him. Turns out, she was late. Randy and I mosied about the grounds, looked out over the Rockcliffe's edge, out to town and to the Mississippi. Eventually we wound our way back into the mansion. There we found Mr. Sloan and Mr. Testa, the judge who liked designer clothes and motorcycles, sitting in leather armchairs in the Rockcliffe's wood-paneled lounge, puffing on cigars. There were splashes of liquor in the two glasses on the little table between them.

"Mr. Finn," says Mr. Sloan, spotting me. "Come on in."

We exchanged greetings with him and Mr. Testa.

"You boys equipped yourselves well tonight," says Mr. Sloan. "Except for the gambling." He smiled a little in Mr. Testa's direction. "That might lose you a vote or two."

"You know how to handle a deck?" asks Mr. Testa.

"Picked it up on the river."

"Picked it up on the river," repeats Mr. Testa, chuckling a little. "River gambling was one of my great grandfather's favorite activities," said he. "He used to take cruises, a few days long, cap the nights with cards, a nip, and a fine cigar."

At that, Mr. Testa took a puff of his cigar. He held the cigar out and eyed it as he exhaled, you know, like folks tend to do. The smell of the cigar wafted toward us. Smelled good, gotta admit. Without thinking, I said, "That's a fine smelling cigar, sir. Seems like ages since I had one."

Mr. Sloan coughed a little upon hearing this and sat up in his chair a bit.

Mr. Testa smiled and said, "Mr. Finn, you're an old soul, an old soul indeed."

Warn't exactly sure what he meant by that. "Thank you," says I.

"You know," adds Mr. Testa. "Speaking of cards. You might very well be a wild one in this competition."

"I agree with that, mister," says Randy, as he sort of pulled at my arm. "Great to talk with you two. My sister texted. She's pulling up. We gotta go."

Mr. Sloan and Mr. Testa waved us goodbye. But as we started to step away, Mr. Testa called out, "Mark." We looked back at him. "For the sake of the competition, I recommend you keep that penchant for the occasional cigar between us."

"Yes, sir," says I.

Outside under the porte-cochere, we watched Sharon roll up the looping drive. Randy said, "I can't believe I'm saying this. But, despite you telling a judge you smoke the occasional cigar, despite us getting caught gambling, and despite you eating a spoonful of butter, I think it was a pretty strong night. I mean, Mrs. Klein isn't voting for either of us anyway. But Mrs. Hawkins didn't seem too upset with the gambling, and I think you made an impression on Mr. Testa, and with his friend Mr. Sloan. We made some dough, too. And you paired with Lucy for the next round. That's a coup. That will immediately raise your standing in the eyes of the judges. Well-played, my friend."

"Who are you going to pair with?" asks I.

"Charlotte would be strategic now that Lucy is taken, but I'm sure she'll go with Parker. I couldn't deal with her, anyway. I think Stacey."

Randy's sister greeted us through the window. Randy stepped around to get in the car.

"I'm not driving you home?" asked she of me.

"Nah," says I, looking up at the sky. "It's a beautiful night. I'm walking."

She stared at me for several moments.

"You are an odd duck," said she. "Well, how did it go, you two?"

Standing by the passenger side, Randy leaned through the car window and said, "We got caught gambling and Mark ate butter, oh, and he talked about his cigar-smoking with Mr. Testa."

"What!?" asked she. "These are not things we prepped for."

"And yet," says Randy, "I actually think it was a strong night for both of us."

"You both are very odd," says Sharon.

———

I walked to Orion's. He'd given me the code for his front door. So I entered it, strolled in, and hollered hello. Found him tinkering.

"Good to see you, Mark," says he, crouched between two tables, staring at a snaggle of small gears, a hinge, and what looked like a horizontal gate, all of which was super-illuminated by the flashlight strapped to his forehead. Tools and parts were strewn about, among them balloons and tracks and pulleys. One of the two tables he was working between stood about half the height of a regular table, the other was at regular height. He discarded a tool, grabbed another, then stared at me blankly for a few moments.

"Oh," says I, realizing that he was confused by my outfit. "We had that formal dinner tonight."

"That's right," says he. "Yes, of course."

"Why the flashlight strapped to your forehead?"

"Ah, my eyes—and the lighting in here. How'd the dinner go?"

"It was interesting," says I. "I think plenty good."

He leaned between the tables again.

"Can you hold this hinge right here?" asks he. "I need to fasten it."

"Sure."

Working, he asked, "So, who'd you sit with?"

"Lucy Thoreau."

"Is that so?"

"Yes. And I sat next to a jeweler..."

"Mr. Sloan."

"That's right."

"Any judges at your table?"

"Mr. Smullens, the economics guy. And Mrs. Klein, the hoity-toity one."

Orion smiled. "Tough."

"Yes, but Mr. Sloan warn't bad. He's the one that suggested Lucy and I pair up for a new feature of the competition, acting out a Tom and Becky scene."

"Lucy's your partner?"

"Yes."

"She's nice?"

"She is. And she's beautiful."

I hadn't really meant to say it, it'd just sprung out. I didn't want people to know of my feelings for Lucy as of yet.

He stood up and stepped back to analyze his machine, then put a stool between the two tables. Atop of this stool he placed a rubber mat and on top of that a hotplate, which was plugged in. Next, he fastened a small, uninflated balloon to a metal prong which he positioned jest above the hot plate. I spotted a carton of eggs off to the side of the tables. *This is one peculiar contraption*, thunk I.

Continuing to work, he asked, "Mark, what is driving you to be Tom?"

"Well, I can't say with certainty—it seems fun, you know, being Tom. He's a one-of-a-kind character. And maybe I want to participate in something that regular kids get to do."

"Your parents, life on the farm, doesn't allow for much of that, uh?"

"That's right."

Orion stepped back to gaze again at the contraption. "I think we got this part squared away."

He picked up an egg and placed it at the start of a track. The egg wobbled down the looping decline till *smack!* it hit the edge of a skinny gate. The gate's edge cracked the egg while the egg's force pushed open the gate. The yolk dropped free of the gate and fell onto the hot plate below, within centimeters of the uninflated balloon rigged above the plate. When the egg hit the skillet, it started frying. And as it fried, steam rose off the egg. This steam made the balloon expand. The balloon got bigger and bigger for a good minute till it went *pop!* and the air rushed out of it. The force of this air started a ping pong ball along a separate track on the lower table.

"Bingo!" says Orion, nodding approvingly. "Velocity, gravity, hot air, cool air, steam, pressure. So much at play. Now, let's take a break."

At the kitchen island, Orion asked further about the dinner. I told him of the butter and of the gambling and of the cigar conversation with Mr. Testa and Mr. Sloan in the lounge.

He could only chuckle and shake his head.

"Mr. Sloan, he's a solid man," Orion said. "Has influence, too. Owns a lot of gold. Land as well. He's level-headed, though, not snooty and status-minded. Good one to have on your side." Orion paused a few moments. "Any murmurings of the Dr. Knotts fella at the dinner?"

"No," said I. "Why, are there new developments?"

"Well, we asked him to donate the Huckleberry Finn items to the museum. Have been waiting on a response, which he apparently gave today."

"Oh, yeah?"

"He declined the request. Instead, now that he can prove his find, he said he's going to auction the items through Sotheby's, on a livestream. He offered to pay the museum a fee to host the stream here in St. Petersburg, at the museum."

My, thunk I. "What'd the museum folks say?"

"The fee he's willing to pay is quite high. The museum is strapped for cash as is. I think they'll accept."

"When do you think this would happen?"

Orion looked at me for a few moments. "Sounds like he wants to do it in a couple of weeks, maybe sooner."

My throat gulped.

"And the museum, I mean, you think it's a good idea to team up with Dr. Knotts?"

Orion eyed me. "Have you heard of this Dr. Knotts before?"

"Me, oh no," says I, feigning. "No, he jest sounds ruther peculiar."

"He is," says Orion. "I've been thinking a lot about the whole scenario. Rather uncommon."

On my walk back to Pap's, the stars shone bright through a deep dark. I let my mind wander. Back at the cabin, lying on my bearskin, the stillness of the night permeated right through me and eased my nerves. A small fire kept me warm. After a while I picked up L'Amour and read up on the Sacketts. The idea of heading West like they did, to build a life unencumbered, seemed especially appealing now with Dr. Knotts coming back. *You've* got to win *Lucy first*, says I to myself. *To do that, you need to see this competition through, while dodging Dr. Knotts, and the govment for that matter.*

Warn't gonna be easy.

CHAPTER THIRTEEN

I let a few days run along before I ventured out of the forest to meet Randy on his walk home from school.

"Mark," says he, anxiously, as I approached. "Where have you been, for crying out loud?"

"Oh, jest at home, you know, getting homeschooled," says I.

"You, my friend, are entirely too nonchalant. You need to connect with Lucy, like now. Are you mad? I mean, you two get paired and then you go dark. Rumor at school today was, with you AWOL, Parker-Wallace might drop his partner and make a run at Lucy."

I had no idea.

Randy continued, "I was wracking my brain, trying to figure out how to reach you. And I realized there's no way to do so. Do you have a phone?"

"No," stretched I. Technically, I had that burner Ned borrowed me, but I hadn't used it.

"No phone at all—like not even an old school house phone?"

"My parents are really old-fashioned."

"Okay, we'll just have to schedule meet-ups better. You can't just disappear. Anyway, speaking of scheduling, we need to plan out the rest of the competition. But first, you need to go to Lucy's house right now and invite her to work with you on the Tom and Becky scene."

"You mean invite her to where I live?"

"Yes, over to your house. All the other boys have done so with their partners. It's already like a thing. This is the first year for acting out scenes and already the expectation is we're supposed to ask the girl over to work on the scene."

"Did you do that?"

"Yes. And you need to ride to Lucy's now and do the same."

"Okay, okay," says I.

"Then come by for dinner. We can map out our game plan. And my little brother says he wants to see more magic."

"Sure," says I. "I'll come to dinner."

"You'll stop by Lucy's first?"

"Yes, I'll do that," says I, hesitantly.

He looked at me confused. "Are you sure you're going to do that?"

"Listen," says I, leaning toward Randy. "I can't exactly bring her to my house."

"Why not?" asks he.

"It's jest that…it's…as I say, my parents keep to themselves. They aren't social. They don't see much of anybody."

"Oh yeah," says Randy. "No problem. Practice at my place."

"Would it be all right?"

"Absolutely. My mom will be good with it. She'll love it. Sharon will, too. You need to do this. You cannot let Parker-Wallace swoop in and get Lucy. Do you hear me?"

Riding to Lucy's, I couldn't help but notice the crumbling edges of sidewalk along Hill Street, or how at some points the sidewalk simply stopped only to pick up again a bit later, or how the stone retaining walls out in front of many of the homes were crumbling. Sure, there were some powerful grand homes, like the Rockcliffe and Lucy's. But a lot needed tending.

Took a deep breath walking up to the Thoreau's wide front porch. The knocker for the front door was in the form of a cast iron lion which stared back at me ruther imposing-like. I pulled it up so it could swing down and alert the Thoreaus of my presence. Lucy's dad came to the door.

He wore a fine suit; seemed a bit surprised to see me. His eyes landed on my moccasins. I looked down at 'em and saw the frayed ends of my cut-off cargoes as well. Looking back up, I just kinda shrugged. "I was hoping to talk to Lucy a minute."

"Is that so?" asks he. "What's your name?"

"Finn, Mark Finn," says I. We'd met. I'd reckoned he knew me. "And, um, we've partnered to perform a Tom and Becky scene. I'm wondering if Lucy would like to work on it."

Becky came into view behind him. She waved as she stepped to the door. "Hello, Mark," says she.

Her dad stared a few moments, almost through me. He glanced Lucy's direction, saying, "I thought you hadn't heard from your partner?"

"Well, not until now," says she.

"I'm new to this, you see," says I to both of 'em. "Being homeschooled and living out on the farm and not having a phone, well, I didn't know exactly what was expected, as far as preparing for the scene and all."

"You don't have a phone?" asked her dad.

"I think I have a burner phone, but I haven't used it." He looked at me like I was missing cards.

"I liked the idea of no phone better than a burner phone," says he. "Why do you need a burner phone?"

"Sir, I don't know hay about phones. Don't use 'em much. Is it bad to have a burner phone?"

He eyed me.

"C'mon, Dad," says Lucy.

"Where exactly do you two plan on practicing?" asked he.

"Dad," says she again. "We haven't even had a chance to talk."

"Speaking of that," says I, leaning to the side to better see Lucy. "I was thinking that ruther than travel all the way out to my mam and pap's farm, it'd be easiest to practice at Randy's. My mam and pap kinda keep to themselves nohow."

"A friend's place?" interjected Lucy's dad.

"Randy Walker's," says I. "Do you know him?"

"No."

"Yes, you do, Dad," interjects Lucy. "He's in my grade. You met him last year at the school play. He's a Tom finalist, too. And you've met Mark before."

"I have?"

"Yes, in the caves."

"The caves…oh, were you the young man who sort of popped up out of nowhere and said you were from the bottom of Arkansaw?"

"Yes, sir," says I.

He looked perplexed.

"Can we practice at Randy's?" asks Lucy to her dad.

"I'll have to meet his parents."

"Great," says I. "Well, it's jest his ma. Pap's not around. Might tomorrow evening work, seven o'clock?" asked I, looking toward Lucy.

"I'll bring her by," says Lucy's pap.

I nodded and started down the porch before turning back, "Lucy, I meant to ask," says I. "What scene do you have mind?"

"I'm thinking the cave scene," says she. "Seems like the most dramatic."

"That'll work. See you tomorrow."

———

With Lucy having agreed to practice our scene, my ride back to Randy's for dinner felt like a breeze. Rolling up, I found his little brother Mikey playing basketball out front. Randy welcomed me in.

"How'd it go?"

"Good."

"Good? Just good? Did you set up a time for her to come over and practice the scene?" asked he, turning on the TV.

"Yes, well sort of…"

"Sort of?"

"Her Dad said he's going to bring her by tomorrow at seven o'clock. He wants to meet your mom. Did you ask her if it's all right for us to practice at your place?"

"It's fine."

We sat on the couch and Randy put on a show called *Seinfeld.* He was shocked I'd never heard of it. "It's like you're from a different planet," said he.

While we watched, he described the show's different characters to me. I appreciated his enthusiasm but found myself scratching my head—I mean, the show warn't about nothing, far as I could tell.

By and by Randy's mom called for us to help set the table. Mikey and sister Sharon joined us.

"What's the update?" asks Sharon to Randy, in a way that let me know she was aware of the Parker-Wallace rumor.

"Well," says Randy. "Mr. Finn here went over to Lucy's to set up a time to practice and she agreed to it."

"Good," says Sharon.

"And they're going to practice here, tomorrow night," Randy said.

"Happy to have you," said Randy's mom. Whew, thunk I, looking over at Randy—it sounded like he hadn't even asked.

"It's so exciting," says Sharon. "I get to direct two scenes."

Randy rolled his eyes.

We talked a bit more about the competition. Unexpectedly, Randy's mom brought up the Huck Finn artifacts that had been "found" by Dr. Knotts.

"Have you all talked about it at school?" asks she. "It was in the paper today."

That caught my attention.

"My history teacher mentioned something about it," says Sharon.

"Orion told me," says I.

"Orion Halley?" asked Randy's mom, surprised.

I hesitated a moment, thinking maybe I shouldn't've brung him up. "Yes, ma'am," says I.

"You know him?" asked she.

"Yes. I help him time to time with star-mapping and his Rube Goldberg machines."

"Who?" asks Sharon. "What are Rube Goldberg machines?"

"He's the older guy, silver hair, that volunteers at the Tom and Huck museum, kind of eccentric," says Sheila.

"Oh, yeah, wears glasses, hair stands straight up?" says Sharon.

"His family—parents, grandparents—are from this area. Several decades ago they owned a shoe factory in St. Petersburg, along with the Smullens family."

"Same family of my econ teacher, the Tom and Becky judge?" asks Sharon.

"Yes," says Randy's mom. "It shuttered some time ago. Messy process, I think. Led to a falling out. Afterward, Orion got into cement production or something." She paused a few moments, trying to remember. "He became a rather successful sort of scientist-engineer, I think in the automobile industry, too. Word is he invented several products and may still hold patents. He's like an underground genius. Eccentric. Interesting guy. Lost his wife a few years ago. Quite sad. A wonderful woman, by all accounts." She looked at me. "What does Orion think of the Huck Finn artifacts?"

"Uh, he hasn't really said much," stated I, "other than the DNA tests came back positive, meaning that the artifacts was indeed Huck's. And now the fella who has them, Dr. Knotts, wants to auction 'em off. Oh, and Orion said the Knotts fella is willing to pay a considerable fee to have the auction in St. Petersburg, at the B&B Theater."

"Fascinating," says Randy's mom. "How in the world did he come across Huckleberry Finn artifacts? Stories like this don't come to our town too often."

"Speaking of mysterious," says Randy's sister. "You're kind of mysterious, Mark. I mean, you pop up all of a sudden, seemingly out of nowhere, and you know eccentric people like Orion Halley. I don't even know him, and I've lived here my whole life."

I shrugged.

"Yep, you're an enigma," continued she.

"Sharon," said Randy's mom, in a tone suggesting she ease up.

"I don't mean that in a bad way. I'm just saying. He's mysterious." She turned to me. "Regardless, I'm excited to direct your scene with Lucy."

"I wouldn't say you're exactly the director," juts in Randy.

Sharon rolled her eyes. "Don't be silly," said she. "Listen boys, we need to do run-throughs tonight." She looked at me. "Mark, what scene am I directing for you and Lucy?"

"Lucy mentioned the one during which Tom and Becky get lost in the cave," said I.

"Love it," says Sharon. "As you probably know, Randy and Stacey are doing the scene in which Tom takes a whooping on Becky's behalf." She tapped Randy on the shoulder and smiled. "Very noble."

Prior to running-through our scenes with Sharon, Mikey asked for some magic.

"Sure," says I. "Do you have a sheet of paper I can borrow?"

He fetched a sheet and handed it to me. Randy and Sharon seemed as eager as Mikey to see what I had in mind.

"Okay, okay, wait a second," said I, getting up from the table. I walked to the kitchen to grab plastic cups. Returning to the dining room, I took a seat at the table and asked them to sit across from me.

"This trick is called the Permeation."

On my way to the kitchen, on the sly, I'd ripped the paper into three parts and crumpled each into a ball. Sitting across from them now, I put the cups down, in a row, jest like you might if you were going to pour something into them. I had them look into the cups to confirm they were empty.

"I have two paper balls here," says I, not revealing the third which was hidden from their view, tucked as it was between the little pocket that forms when you bring your thumb and index finger together.

I proceeded to overturn the cups, one in such a fashion that I could sneak the hidden paper ball under it as I placed the cup lip down on the table. Then I placed one of the paper balls atop this cup. "Now," continued I, holding a paper ball for them to see, "I'm gonna show you that I can make this paper ball, setting atop this here overturned cup, magically permeate through the base of the cup and end up underneath it." I took a second cup and stacked it atop the first, moved my hands over the stacked cups as if conjuring some wild magic, and, *voilà* pulled up the two stacked cups to reveal the paper ball resting on the table underneath.

Mikey's jaw dropped. Randy and Sharon were wowed, too.

"Now, wait a minute," says Sharon. "How'd you do that?"

"Well, if the conditions are right," says I, pulling the two stacked cups apart. "I could maybe do it again."

"Yes," says Mikey.

"Okay, Mikey," says I. "I'm going to try to give the paper ball I jest revealed to you a buddy." I showed them both cups, one of them now with a paper ball at the bottom, which they could see. Then I overturned the cups again, tilting the one already holding a paper ball, so that I could again sneak a paper ball under its lip. I put a different paper ball atop the cup like before and stacked a cup over it. Made some mystic-like motions with my arms and hands, pretended to listen to the stacked cups, and, *voilà*, lifted them to reveal two paper balls now sitting next to each other on the table.

"Look at that!" says Mikey. "There's two!"

"What do you know?" asks Randy.

"Now how'd he do that?" wondered Sharon.

"I don't know," says Mikey.

"It's called Permeation," said I, smiling.

"You're a magician," says Sharon. "Plain and simple. The man knows magic. And it's going to take some magic to pull these scenes off. The director says it's time to get to work."

"For tomorrow, by the way, when Lucy and Stacey come to practice, they don't know that you think you're the director," says Randy.

"I'll have a word with them later," says Sharon.

"Before you do anything," says Randy's ma, stepping in from the kitchen. "The dishes aren't going to magically clean themselves."

"We got it," says Randy.

After dishes, Randy and his sister brung me into the living room to learn me tricks of the acting trade. Sharon acted out the cave scene with me as if she were Lucy. We ran through it several times. Both Randy and Sharon had done several school plays and offered me insight on how to position my body to the audience, on projecting my voice, on hitting marks, and the like. It helped.

Randy and Sharon practiced his scene next. I couldn't offer much as far as tips, jest told him it seemed awful good. And it did. Sharon seemed pleased, declared us at least presentable.

Randy walked with me out to the driveway. "Hey, Mark," said he. "Maybe I can come to your place, and together we could talk to your parents about the competition, get them to get behind it? It's a bummer they aren't supporting you."

Randy'd been so kind to me, helpful in all sorts of ways. I didn't want to tell him any more stretchers. "Well, it's ruther complicated," says I.

"How so?" asks Randy.

"Thing is, I ain't got no parents."

"What?" asks he. "Seriously?"

"I don't got parents."

Randy paused a few moments. "I'm sorry to hear that, Mark. Who do you live with?"

"You need to promise to keep this betwixt us."

"Okay, betwixt us," says Randy, cracking a smile.

"I live alone."

"You live alone?"

"Yes."

"Where?"

I warn't ready to go whole hog. "A farm out yonder," says I, waving an arm in the general direction.

"Out yonder? You gotta show me this place. I mean, this is incredible. I've never known anyone our age who lives on their own."

"I can show you some time," says I vaguely.

"What happened to your parents, if you don't mind me asking?"

"They're dead," says I. "My mom fell ill when I was young. And my pap, he was a drunk, got murdered."

"Man," says Randy. "Well, my dad's basically a drunk, too, if it makes you feel any better." He paused a few moments. "I can't believe you live alone. This weekend, can you show me where you live?"

"Sure," says I.

Randy looked back at his house. "You know, Mark, I can check with my mom and see if you can stay here."

"No, I'm used to being on my own. Plus, I don't want no fuss. Govment will try to stick its nose in, and all kind of problems ensue. Appreciate it, but jest keep this betwixt us."

Randy nodded and I pushed on.

I warn't exactly sure why I told him other than, as I say, being grateful for our friendship and for him accepting me and opening his home to me. I judged he warn't gonna tell no one.

———

Next evening, I rolled back over to Randy's on the Spacelander. Randy and his family greeted me warmly. Me and him and Sharon talked about the scene. When Lucy and her pap rung, we all come to the door. I's a bit nervous. Randy's mom welcomed them in. Lucy looked beautiful as ever. She was easy to cotton to.

"It's good to meet you all," says Lucy's pap, exchanging greetings.

"We're excited Mark and Lucy are going to practice their scene here," says Randy's mom. "Sharon, I'm sure, will give them any help they need, whether they want it or not."

Lucy's pap smiled and said, "Thank you." Looking at Lucy, he added, "I'll be back in an hour and a half."

Lucy and I and Randy and Sharon spilled into the family room.

"Welcome to our home," says Sharon.

"It's lovely," says Lucy.

We talked of the competition and the judges as Sharon put Lucy's hair in braids then tied on a ribbon, like Becky'd done in the *Adventures of Tom Sawyer.* Randy fetched a candle for the cave scene and gave it to Lucy. She seemed to be deep in thought. Then she sort of come to and said that she jest had the idea of us doing the scene without words.

Randy and Sharon thought about it a few moments.

"I like it," says Randy.

"*Avant-garde,*" agreed Sharon. "Let's try it."

I warn't sure what avant-garde meant, but I was fine with it if Lucy was for it.

Lucy and me begun the scene by acting as if we's walking in the cave with our schoolmates, gazing at the cave walls. By and by, I take her by the hand and we slide aside as if we's peeling off from the class, to go exploring. We marvel at stalactites here, wind through a passage there, all by weaving back and forth in Randy's living room. I felt awful silly but Lucy held character and that helped me keep form. Sharon and Randy stopped matters on occasion to give direction, mainly to offer a tip to help me get right.

Next, the bats fly in and we take off running from one side of the living room to the other, waving our arms, frightened as can be. Lucy's braids come undone and her ribbon drops to the floor, a touch which Randy and Sharon said they's all for.

Now we are lost. We search and search for a way out. A day seems to pass but have no way to tell. Worn out, we find a spring, sit by it. Powerful exhausted, we fall out. We arise facing long odds. With Becky resting, I drag myself through the cave to again seek a way out, only to recoil in shock upon discovering that the real murderer of Dr. Robinson is hiding out in the cave.

We practiced these parts of the scene several times till Sharon and Randy declared themselves satisfied.

The final portion of the scene features Tom and Becky facing near death, their energy depleted, hope nearly gone. Becky and I pretend to wearily sip water at a spring. Resigned to a seemingly tragic fate, we eke out the energy to write our names on the cave wall so folks would know who we was when they find our dead skeletons.

With life nearly sapped out of us, I pull out the sliver of cake I'd saved and give it to Becky. She splits it and hands half back to me, perhaps our last meal before perishing. Somehow I muster the energy to search one last time for a way out and lo and behold, this time I find a speck of light at the end of a small passageway. I go back for Becky and bring her to it. We squeeze through the opening and embrace on the other side.

"Bravo." Sharon clapped.

"That's good," says Randy.

"Only thing I'd add," says Sharon, "at the very end, you two could look at the light and say 'Freedom'—the only word either of you speak the whole time."

A knock sounded at the front door. 'Twas Lucy's father. Seemed like ten minutes had swum by, yet an hour and a half had passed. Ain't that how it is? When bored, time moves slower than sap. Lucy comes over, it moves faster than lightning.

Randy's mom got to the door first. "They worked the entire time," she said. "You'd've been proud. I think you're going to like the scene."

"Good," says Lucy's pap, still ruther stiff.

"Next Thursday, then?" asks I of Lucy before she pushed off.

"Yes, see you then, Mark." says she.

———

Later that night I found Orion in his shop, looking at his ceiling-high starboard. I think he was muttering to himself about the relationship between gravity and time.

"What are you working on?" asks I.

"Oh, nothing," says he. "Just thinking. Great to see you, ole boy. Do you want to skywatch a bit?"

"Sure," says I.

We walked out to the deck off of his upstairs office and each of us sat under a telescope. "Let's see what Mars is up to first. Have I shown you China's Space Lab?"

"I don't think so."

Using his tablet, Orion guided me to a planet cluster which included Mars, Saturn, and Jupiter. He said the moon was in the midst of swinging near this cluster. Through the telescope I could see the sketch he was drawing of the forecasted path.

"You see 'em now?" asks he.

"I do, by golly," says I.

"The moon is going to pull on time a little on its way past the planets. Warp time a little, you understand, and do the same to the gravitational field."

"Warp time, huh?"

"That's right," says Orion, his eyes twinkling. "Now, on to China's space lab." Using his tablet, he circled the lab which allowed me to locate it easily through the scope's field.

"I see it," says I.

"A whole lotta stolen technology up there."

"That so?"

"I worked on some of it. The Chinese government likes to 'borrow' as Huck used to say."

I chuckled.

"Let me show you a special star." Orion shifted my telescope manually and then used his tablet to guide me. "This star," said he, stretching a line out from it, "is on a direct path to hit a black hole."

"A black hole?"

Orion explained black holes and entanglement, which led him to covering time travel.

"Your telling me someone could travel back in time?" asks I.

"Technically, yes, and forward," says he, looking up at the sky. "Don't you believe in time travel?"

I thought on it a few moments. "I guess I do."

"Wormholes make it possible, if the conditions and energy are right. If you think of the universe as an apple and the worm as the traveler, the worm goes through a hole in the universe to get to a new place in time. In this case, the other side of the apple, or universe."

I nodded, only half getting it. We gazed at the sky for a minute or so in silence.

"Speaking of time travel," says Orion. "I had lunch with Dr. Knotts the other day, before he left town."

"That so?"

"The man has some interesting theories. Big ideas."

"Oh, yeah?"

Orion paused a moment and looked at me. "But he's driven by greed and money."

"How do you know?"

"I can tell. Anyway, don't you worry about him, Mark," says Orion, reassuringly, before getting back under his telescope. "He'll run his little auction, and then he'll get out of town."

This left me feeling unsure as to what exactly Orion knew. I mean, the way he said it made me think he knew more than he was saying.

Late that night back at Pap's, lying on my bearskin next to a small fire, I determined that no matter what Orion might suspect or know, he wouldn't use it against me. This made me feel more at ease about matters.

My mind wandered to what Randy had said about not being able to reach me when Parker-Wallace nearly swooped in to be Lucy's acting partner. I judged it time I figured out that burner phone Ned had borrowed me. I dug it out of the Mother Lode and flipped it open and, what do you know, but a letter from Ned slid out. It read:

Huck,

I hope this finds you well. This phone might come in handy. I've written the number for it below. Make sure you keep the battery charged. Can't be "playing Angry Birds all day, eating bonbons," as Coach Rogy would say.
Good luck, my friend,
Ned

Took some fumbling around but eventually I found the right button with which to turn the phone on. As it awoke, I thought about texting Randy, but then I realized I didn't know his number—or anyone else's, for that matter. When it fully loaded, I just sort of stared at it. I's about to turn the burner off when it made a "ping" sound. A message had come in. 'Twas from Ned. He'd sent it weeks prior, looked like. The message was of a general sort, wishing me well, encouraging me to reach out if I needed him. I texted back:

Ned, Thank you for the burner and the message. I'm doing fine. Actually found Pap's old cabin—remember, the one from that Huckleberry Finn book in English class. It's in Missouri, nice and hid. Don't tell no one. Hope you are well. Tell the rest of the Musketeers hello for me.

Mark.

I waited a bit but didn't hear nuthin' back.

CHAPTER FOURTEEN

The following week, Lucy's pap dropped her at Randy's again for practice. We'd decided to practice in full costume this time. Lucy wore hers well, a white frock and embroidered pantalettes, hair plaited into two locks with a ribbon. Sharon had put me in that straw fedora and suspenders and teased my hair with that spray again. She'd done the same to Randy's hair.

Lucy's pap seemed a little more comfortable dropping her off for this practice. In small talk with Randy's mom, he mentioned that it was a particularly good year for the competition given all the hullabaloo over the upcoming auction of Huckleberry Finn items.

"It's remarkable, isn't it?" says Randy's mom. "Are you planning on attending the auction?"

"Indeed," said Lucy's pap.

"The scenario has created quite a stir. The papers say this Dr. Knotts character has proved it's Huck's DNA."

"Yet," said Lucy's pap, "he hasn't said how he got the pipe and other items. He says he will explain matters later and that there's more to come. But I don't understand why he won't just tell us where and how he found the items."

"And what's he mean by more to come?" wondered Randy's ma.

Lucy's pap shrugged in shared bewilderment, then turned to Lucy. "Call me when you're done."

"I can drive her home when we're done, if that helps," says Sharon.

"Or, I can just walk," says Lucy.

"Okay, see you all later."

Randy's partner Stacey arrived. They was set to practice, too. Once we all got situated in the living room, you know, by pushing furniture around to set the stage, Randy and Stacey run through their scene. 'Twas a hoot watching them act it out: Becky seemingly caught tearing a book page, Tom taking the fall. Randy took to acting with natural ease. Stacey played both Becky and the teacher awful good. And the paddling she gave Randy elicited hoots from us. After each run-through, Sharon would throw in her shovel, and they'd talk elements through. They did this a few times.

Lucy and me went next. Took some run-throughs but by and by the scene started rolling right along. As before, Sharon threw in her shovel. After our fourth go, she declared us ready.

"It's really good," says Randy.

"Thank you," said Lucy. "It's nice that we can help each other out even though it's a competition."

"Right here in this room," says Sharon, "we might have the winners of Tom and Becky. And I heard they are going on a trip this fall, maybe Asia. Shanghai anyone? Possibly Europe, London perhaps?"

"Seriously?" asks Lucy.

"A few years ago they sent Tom and Becky to India," says Sharon.

"I've always wanted to go to London," says Lucy.

"Me, too," said Randy. "Get some fish and chips, stop by the Harry Potter set?"

"I was thinking more like Buckingham Palace," says Lucy.

"That robber from there, he always seemed interesting," says I. "What was his name?"

"A famous English robber?" asks Randy, a little puzzled.

"Yeah, you know, he stole from sheriffs and bishops and kings," says I, trying to remember his name.

"You mean Robin Hood," asks Lucy.

"Yes, that's right. Robin Hood."

"I didn't realize he was English."

"You sound like Tom Sawyer right now," says Lucy. "He talks about Robin Hood in the same way."

I shrugged and said, "If I go to England, I think it'd be nice to see Robin Hood's hideout. I hear he hid out deep in the forest, where nobody could get to him."

"That would be something," says Randy, nodding my way, "living on your own out in the wild."

Too soon, time come for Lucy to get back home. She grabbed her sweater and started for the door. Randy waved his arms at me, as if to say "Get going." Sharon smiled and shook her head. Luckily, Lucy didn't seem to notice. I headed for the door.

"I could walk you back," says I to Lucy. She turned toward me and smiled.

"That'd be nice."

I grabbed my moccasins from the Spacelander and slipped 'em on. As we walked, I wheeled the bike along.

"Where did you get that bike?" asked Lucy.

"Orion lent me it," says I.

"The scientist who works at the museum?"

"Yes."

"Seems like an interesting person," says she. "And that is an interesting bike. It looks like a spaceship."

"I think that's what the designer had in mind, least-ways that's what Orion says."

"My bike's rather ordinary."

"Sometimes ordinary is jest fine," says I.

"How do you mean?" asks she.

"Well, you know, sometimes simple and regular, not standing out, is pleasant."

"I don't want ordinary. I like unique things. Like your bike. It's design makes me think of venturing off, and I want to see the world, you know, learn about it, maybe some day study abroad in college, later work overseas. You know, do extraordinary things."

"You think about college?" asks I.

"Yes, don't you?"

"Not so much. Where do you want to go?"

"Notre Dame," says she. "Or Stanford."

"Notre Dame?"

"Yes."

"I know Notre Dame," says I. "I've been there. Touchdown Jesus, the Golden Dome."

"Isn't it beautiful?"

Her love for Notre Dame got me thinking maybe I should try to go there, too. Of course, I hadn't been in school much. Perhaps football could be my ticket, wondered I.

"So, are you Catholic?" asks she.

Nobody ever asked me about being a Papist before. "Can't say I am."

"But your parents like Notre Dame—that's why they took you there?"

I had to wiggle out of this one. "Actually, that's kind of a long story. I have sort of a cousin, you could say, in Indiana. He and his family, the MacSheas, took me there."

"What do you mean, sort of a cousin?"

"Well," stalled I. "The MacSheas are close friends. Really, they're like family. And the dad, Mr. MacShea, he went to Notre Dame. He brung us there when I's visiting."

"My dad went to Notre Dame, too," says she.

"I'm thinking that's where I'd like to go," says I, looking at her. "Maybe play football."

Lucy smiled. "You know, Mark, I can't believe we never met before that day I saw you in the bookshop."

"Well, it warn't long prior that my parents moved us up from Arkansaw," says I.

"Are your parents coming next week, to watch us act out our Tom and Becky scene?"

"No, they don't come out for stuff like that."

"That's a bummer."

"It's all right."

We came upon Lucy's house.

"I'll see you next week, at the theater," says she, turning toward me.

"Yes," says I.

We faced each other, with only the Spacelander between us. A few awkward moments passed. I wanted to lean in and give her a kiss but my legs wobbled and in the back of my mind I saw Lucy's pap coming after me if I tried.

"I had fun working on our scene," says she. "See you soon." She gave me a little wave before turning toward her home.

"Take care now," says I.

Upon alighting the porch steps, she glanced back and waved again. As she opened the door, I saw the silhouette of her father, watching from inside. Made me less regretful that I hadn't tried for a kiss.

CHAPTER FIFTEEN

On the evening that we was to perform our scenes, us Toms and Beckys arrived at the B&B Theater a couple hours early, as did the judges. Randy and I showed up dressed in our costumes, as directed by Sharon. Parker-Wallace and Sterling had a good chuckle at our expense for that, as all the other contestants brought their costumes with them to change into at the B&B.

Museum folks, among 'em Jack, the president, whom Orion had told me of, huddled us together to take us on a tour. They showed us backstage, where scaffolding rose a few stories high, and from which equipment of different sorts hung, among it ropes and pulleys. Strewn about the floor was set props of various kinds. Our guides described the work of stagehands. Next, they walked us downstairs to the space under the stage and showed us there a secret, horizontal door on the ceiling which gave access to the main stage above. For fun, several of us contestants, standing on a wooden box, took turns popping our heads through to look about.

Mrs. Klein, clutching her Nantucket purse close, seemed rather annoyed at us for playing around. Mrs. Brown, the poker-faced judge with no airs, explained that the passageway was used to bring actors onto the stage from a different vantage point or to add a set piece to a scene on the sly.

They took us to a different part of the theater's basement, behind and below the main stage, where there was a large dressing room. Here the museum folks and judges went over particulars, like the order in which we'd be performing our skits, and how we was to enter and exit the stage, and the like.

By and by a few hairdressers come in through the back entrance. Mrs. Hawkins explained that they worked for the shop at which she got her hair done and that they were her girlfriends and had agreed to do hair touch-up for us, even makeup. Randy guided me to a chair and told the hairdresser stationed at it, "Let's start with him."

The hairdresser smiled and got to work. Another set to work on Randy. Those not getting worked on went into changing rooms to get into costume. 'Twas hard to tell the Toms apart, the Beckys too, once we was all in costume and done up.

While the hairdresser who'd worked on my hair was finishing with Lucy's, Judge "Sunk Cost" Smullens come over and struck up a conversation with me.

"Your costume looks spot on, Mark."

"Thank you."

"Are you excited about the prospect of becoming Tom?"

"Sounds bully," says I. I didn't mention that I warn't interested if Lucy warn't Becky.

"I'll bet your parents are, too?" says he.

"Sure are," says I.

"Are they here tonight?"

"Might be," stretched I.

"I'd love to meet 'em. Maybe you can introduce me to them after the show?"

"Umm, sure," says I. "Thing is, they generally keep to themselves, so it's not likely they'll be here. But if they are…"

"They keep to themselves?"

I's about to answer when Mr. Testa chimed in.

"My dad didn't attend things like this, either," says he. "Don't worry about it, Mark."

Judge Smullens started to say something, but Mrs. Hawkins called for the judges to head back up to the main theater.

They had Lucy and me going last; Randy and Stacey jest before us. This gave us time to chat in the dressing room while the other contestants went up to get set to perform. Time to time, while waiting, we practiced parts of our scenes, but mainly we chewed the fat. Randy had no end to humorous observations and analysis. He and Stacey made a good pair. And talking with Lucy was more comfortable-like.

By and by, we headed upstairs, bound for a little waiting area off to the side of the main stage. In the hallway, I spotted Orion walking toward me. At first, he didn't seem to recognize me, what with my costume and all. But when I got close and waved, he said, "Hello there, Mark." I introduced him to Lucy.

"Lucy, it is a pleasure," says Orion, shaking her hand. "I'm excited to watch the show." He turned to me. "Mr. Finn, do you mind if I have a quick word with you?"

"Sure," says I, stepping over, unsure what to think.

He sort of huddled me off to the side.

"What is it?" asked I.

"Well, Mark," says he, "I don't aim to get too into your business, you understand, but I wanted to let you know that Dr. Knotts will be here tonight. He wants to get a feel for the venue before his auction tomorrow. I'm not sure what you'll want to do with this information, if anything. I just wanted you to have it. And, remember, if you need anything, just let me know."

I took a deep breath. "Thank you, Orion," says I. "I'm still going to go on stage."

"Well, good. Knock 'em dead," said he, before turning and heading back down the hall.

I stepped over to Lucy, trying to play nonchalant but knowing I's knee-deep in pickle juice. Maybe Dr. Knotts won't recognize me in my Tom costume, says I ruther unconvincingly to myself.

A parade of dignitaries addressed the crowd before our performances. When the pomp wrapped,

Parker-Wallace and Charlotte, then Sterling and Jessica acted out their scenes. From our vantage, side-stage, they performed their scenes admirably, must admit.

When Randy and Stacey got called to perform, Lucy and I inched ourselves nearer the edge of the stage to watch. From this vantage, we could see a good portion of the crowd, while it couldn't really see us. I scanned for Dr. Knotts and spotted him near the front, in the middle. He was leaning to his side, talking quietly to that Jack fella, the head of the Tom and Huck Museum, who sat next to him. Looked like a couple of Dr. Knotts's henchmen sat on either side of them.

I sensed Lucy turning to me. "You look like you've seen a ghost," whispered she.

"No, no, it's just...I just...it's nothing," whispered I.

My mind begun to race. I looked to the stage. Randy and Stacey had begun their scene. I reminded myself that we were all in costume.

"They're doing good," whispered Lucy, nodding toward Randy and Stacey.

I gulped and nodded.

"Mark, are you all right? You nervous?"

"No, not really," says I, keeping my voice at a whisper.

"It's going to be fine," said Lucy, reassuringly, rubbing the top of my hand. "Don't worry."

"Thanks," says I. Right then a plan barrelled to mind. "We've got this," says I to Lucy.

Randy and Stacey finished to loud cheers and bowed as the curtain come down. Stagehands quickly changed out the schoolhouse set for the cave backdrop. Then motioned Lucy and me to the stage.

Lucy and I stood side-by-side as the curtain rose for our scene. The lights blinded me a bit. 'Twas hard to see the crowd out in front of us. I didn't know if I wanted to see Dr. Knotts nohow. Lucy and I stood motionless for several seconds. Sharon said this would build drama. Then we begun, making as if we were walking with our class into a cave. We broke away, moving across the stage, looking about, cowering a little, pointing at the cave walls. As the scene unfolded, Lucy's talent for acting shone forth, I could feel it. She glided across the stage, trembling here, showing resolve there, expressing all the emotions that come with facing near death in a cave. And the part of the scene during which I recoiled in horror at eying the murderer who was hiding out seemed to go well, too. The crowd was engaged, I sensed it. A time or two, with my eyes more accustomed to the lighting, I caught a glimpse of Dr. Knotts. Seemed like he was staring at me.

Near the end of the scene, as I pulled out the bit of cake that we was to share after days of near-starvation and with hope nearly gone, my eyes looked out to the crowd and landed on Dr. Knotts. He had the playbill up near his eyes. He leaned in toward one of his henchmen and pointed to it and then our eyes locked. He's onto me, judged I. I sensed Lucy waiting on me. My attention returned to the scene jest in time. I split the cake piece and gave half to Lucy.

As Lucy then lay down, play-acting like she was on death's doorstep, too weak to explore further, I rose up, feigning bone tiredness, making as if I was searching a final time for a way out. As I moved across the stage I saw one of Dr. Knotts's henchmen making his way along a row of seats. He was hunched down a little, trying not to distract spectators. Another of the henchmen was doing the same in the other direction. They's trying to pen me in, realized I.

Moments later, I rejoiced at seeing the light and returned to rouse Lucy and show her. As I helped her to the side of the stage, we paused to look at the proverbial light and declared "Freedom." The curtain dropped and we whisked offstage. The crowd erupted in cheers.

Randy and Stacey patted us on our backs. Moving with pace and guiding Lucy along, we swept our way around to backstage. Reckoned we only had a short time before the henchmen would try to close in.

I took her by the hand and looked into her eyes. We were under the scaffolding.

"You did great," says I.

"You too," says she.

"Lucy, I ain't too good with this stuff. But the truth is, I like you."

She smiled.

"Do you mind if I give you a kiss?" asked I.

She leaned in, and next I knew our lips met and the moon and the stars stopped. For a few quick moments there warn't nothing but Lucy and me. Then *Whoosh!* Dr. Knotts and his henchmen sprang back to mind.

"Listen," says I, looking over my shoulder and taking her by the hands. "This won't make much sense, but I gotta go right now. I'll come find you soon. But right now, I gotta go."

She looked ruther confused, understandably. I pulled away and grabbed hold of a beam of scaffolding above us.

"What are you talking about?" asks she.

"I'll tell you later," said I, continuing to climb up the scaffolding.

Moments later, with me having clumb higher, I heard a hall door open. I looked down toward the sound and saw one of Dr. Knotts's henchmen step into this backstage area. He stared at Lucy and she at him. I froze. He scanned the room but did not see me up above. Thinking all clear, he closed the door and stepped back into the side hall. I continued to climb till I reached the ceiling, several Twains high. Lucy was looking up at me. I pulled myself upon a rafter which run along the ceiling, abreast duct work. I scooted along the rafter till I come to a spot where the duct vented through the roof to outside. Sliding my all-purpose knife out my pocket, I unloosened the duct work paneling and, with some force, popped it free. Then I wiggled my way onto the roof.

Crouching, I quick-stepped to the backside of the building. There I grabbed hold of the fire escape rail and swung down onto the escape steps. I fired my feet down a few flights of steps and hit the ground with my legs a-churning, taking off pell-mell through the alley-way, not looking back till I'd gone over a mile and zig zagged through thick forest.

Didn't stop moving till I made it to Pap's cabin. Exhausted, I popped the cabin door open, aiming to collapse on my bearskin. Only as I come through the door, I stopped dead in my tracks. Someone was inside. My heart nearly leapt out my chest. I strained through the darkness, to see who it was, frightened as can be.

"Mark?" says he. And then I knew.

"By jings! It's you, Ned!" said I.

CHAPTER SIXTEEN

Naturally, Ned wanted to know what I was running from. I told him of Lucy and the Tom and Becky contest, about Orion and Randy, Dr. Knotts and his auction plans, and how Dr. Knotts had jest now figured out I was in town. Ned wanted all the particulars. And his mind went straight to trying to figure out how to help me navigate matters.

Of course, I wanted the rundown on how he came to be at Pap's. The courts, he said, had forced him to spend some school breaks with his pap, on account of his parents' divorce. He couldn't take his pap's drinking no more, especially since his pap tried roughing him up again. And the timing worked out such that shortly after he decided to light out, my text had come through. He caught a Greyhound to St. Petersburg.

"How did you find this cabin?"

"Mark," said Ned, with a glint in his eye. "I mean, we read the *Adventures of Huckleberry Finn* in English class together. And you know me, I did some research and figured it out. Well, also, full disclosure, I downloaded a general location tracker to the burner, thinking it could come in handy were you to get in a tight spot." He shrugged. "I hope you don't mind."

"I'm glad you found me," says I. "I missed you and the rest of the Musketeers."

Ned pulled out his laptop, connected it with a satellite, using some untraceable method, so he said, and set to doing Ned-type things: he found Lucy's Instagram page and an article on the auction and learned that Orion had indeed been quite the businessman some years ago and still owned patents. While he worked, he asked me questions, had me run through every detail of what was happening with the competition, who the judges were, what the next part of the contest entailed. There was less than a week till the picnic. And a day after that would be the official ceremony to name Tom and Becky. He analyzed matters from different angles. The Dr. Knotts auction really grabbed his attention.

"What's going on, Mark, with you and Dr. Knotts?"

I warn't sure how to answer exactly.

Ned continued, "I found a couple of articles on the guy in an obscure, kind of backchannel database. It looks like Dr. Knotts has wealth, partly inherited. He does vague research on global warming..."

"That's a front," says I.

"At the same time, he might be connected to oil interests…"

"That's the ticket."

"He aims to bring extinct animals back to life, too, like the Wooly Mammoth?"

I nodded.

"What's the connection between you two?" asked Ned again.

"I think he knows that I know his global warming research, while government funded, is really a cover for his oil and mineral exploration and for his animal work."

"I don't know. It just seems like there's more to it."

"I suppose he thinks he's kinda my guardian, too," added I.

"Wait, what?" exclaimed Ned. "Like is he your dad?"

"No, no, no, no."

I could tell he had his suspicions. "Look, I'm your friend. So it doesn't really matter. You don't want him to find you for whatever reason. I'm going to help you keep him from doing so."

I appreciated him not pushing me on it.

Ned sent an "encrypted" message to his mom telling her everything was fine except that his dad had been roughing him up and that he'd decided to flee to a friend's place. He wrote that he'd be home in a week and not to worry. Of course, he knew she'd worry. Still, he figured reaching out would at least buy him a little time. He also sent a message to Johnny MacShea, told him he'd found me and that he could tell his parents I was doing fine. Ned said the MacSheas talked of me often.

Next, he sent a message to his dad. He explained matter of fact what he'd done, told his pap that his mom was well aware and said that as far as he was concerned they were done with having any sort of relationship.

Later that night, with a fire to warm us, we talked further. We agreed that Dr. Knotts probably didn't know anything about my cabin. Otherwise, he'd've had it visited by now. To fortify it, jest in case, we built another set of notches on the interior wall, either side of the door, to make it even harder to force open.

Still, we determined we needed an escape hatch in case of a jam. We settled on digging a tunnel from a corner of the cabin out to a nearby snaggle of bushes. Ned rode the Spacelander to Walmart and bought two shovels for the job.

Next night, we went to digging. 'Twas hard labor, but good to chat with Ned whilst doing it. He caught me up on the other Musketeers, Johnny and Tank, and on Rolling Dunes in general. He said that from time to time Family Services popped in on the MacSheas to ask if they'd heard from me. He asked all about how I got to St. Petersburg. I told of traveling through the night and making the bottom of Chicago, bone-tired, of catching the Greyhound, dodging Dr. Knotts's henchman, and spending the night at the Lincoln Museum before hopping a freighter to here.

When we'd dug a hole about four feet deep, we started a-digging horizontal, under the cabin. We dug deep into the night. Hungry and wore out, a short time before the sun awoke, we snuck through the forest to my lines. Pulled off a few fish and brung 'em back to the cabin, to cook 'em and open some snacks. Full, we fell out, slept powerful late.

———

Ned and I spent the next day much the same. I was happy as a pig in mud jest having him around. He seemed to like it at Pap's, other than worrying about his ma. Each morn, he sent her an encrypted message, letting her know he was fine, hoping to ease her nerves. He liked discussing the Tom and Becky contest. Ned relishes a good competition and, as I say, the intrigue of the Dr. Knotts angle fascinated him. He mentioned finding an article online that said the first auction of Huck Finn items had yielded big bids.

"First auction? There's gonna be a second?" asked I.

He kept reading.

"Looks like it. Says here Dr. Knotts pulled a couple items, declared a second auction for them soon, with a teaser that there could be a huge announcement forthcoming."

I knew right away what Dr. Knotts wanted: to out me and have me join him for this second auction. Make him a boatload of cash.

In the afternoon, I scooted out the woods and found Randy on his walk home from school.

"Mark, my goodness, where have you been?" asks he.

"I had to lay low," says I.

"Had to lay low!? You zipped out of the theater like a madman—someone said they thought perhaps by climbing up the backstage scaffolding and through the ceiling onto the roof? I told 'em they're nuts. I mean, that seems crazy. You aren't actually Spider-Man are you?"

I shook my head no.

"I don't know, maybe you are," said Randy. "What I do know is we couldn't find you after your performance—you and Lucy won Best Scene, by the way. Congratulations. And no one has heard so much as boo from you till right now. Do you know how upset Lucy is?"

We stepped inside his house.

"She's upset?" asked I.

"Yes."

"I did tell her I had to go. I knew she probably wouldn't fully understand. But I...wait a minute, did you say we won top scene?"

"Yes."

"That's buckets."

"Buckets?"

"Oh, sorry, that's something some buddies of mine, the Musketeers, say. Means bully, or great."

"Yes, it's buckets," says Randy. "But do you get it?"

"Get what?"

"You can't just go AWOL—a second time no less. Meantime, Parker-Wallace's folks and Sterling's are claiming you don't have parents on a farm in this county or perhaps any other county for that matter. They're saying you're a fraud, that you're ineligible for the competition."

"Their parents said that?"

"They're claiming you shouldn't even be allowed in the finals, which you made by the way, announced yesterday."

"Yesterday? I thought that was today. Did Lucy make it?"

"Yes."

"Awesome. You and Stacey?"

"Yes," says Randy.

"That's buckets."

"Thank you," says Randy. "So too did Parker-Wallace and Charlotte and Sterling Lewis and Jessica Tompkins. Eight left, four boys, four girls. But as I say Parker-Wallace's parents and Sterling's and apparently Charlotte's, and who knows whose else's, are trying to get the judges to disqualify you. They're meeting tonight at the museum."

"Well, I'll..." says I.

Randy looked perplexed. "What's going on, man?"

"Listen," says I, "you know that doctor who ran the auction on those Huckleberry Finn items?"

"Yes, I've read up on it in the papers. Apparently, he made a lot of money at the auction, but last minute pulled some items; said he was saving 'em for a second auction to be held after the naming of Tom and Becky, and that before this next auction he aimed to make a big announcement related to the items. Whole thing's kinda wild."

"Well, that guy, and his henchmen, are looking for me, and I don't want them to get me. He showed up at the theater. I had to sneak out."

"Wow. Really?"

I nodded.

"Okay," says Randy. "Thanks for letting me know. This makes more sense now." He paused several moments to gather his thoughts. "Why does he want to get you?"

"It's just that he…"

"Is he your dad?"

"No. He's not. But I think he wants to be. It's hard to explain."

"You've got to talk to Lucy," said Randy. "Her dad is cozying up to the Parker-Wallace crew. She's confused. She feels like you told her you had parents out on a farm and a bunch of siblings, did you tell her you had six siblings."

Reluctantly, I nodded.

"Do you have six siblings?"

Reluctantly, I shook my head no.

Randy jest shook his head and chuckled a little. "Anyway, now she's wondering if anything you've told her is true, which actually is understandable."

I sat down to think things through.

Randy continued, "The picnic is in two days, day after that Tom and Becky get named. You gotta square things away with Lucy, and we gotta try to help you stay in the competition."

I nodded. "All while avoiding Dr. Knotts."

"Yea, that too," said Randy. "Can you show me where you live later tonight?"

"Sure," says I.

———

Early that evening I went to Lucy's house. Her pap answered the door. He looked at me disapprovingly.

"Is Lucy here?" asked I. I saw her step into view, down the hall a little, behind her pap. She didn't appear excited to see me.

"She's busy tonight, Mark," says he. "She's not available."

Lucy nodded in agreement. She looked disappointed, unsure. I could tell that, at least for now, she didn't want to talk.

"Okay," says I to her pap. "I understand."

I went to Orion's next. Found him stargazing.

"Mark, I'm glad you came by. We need to talk," said he. "Where have you been?"

"It's a long story."

"Have any of the judges or the folks running the Tom and Becky contest been in touch with you recently?"

"No," said I.

"Good," says he.

"Of course, 'tain't easy for 'em to get in touch with me. Why do you ask?"

"Parents of some contestants have filed a complaint with contest officials. Apparently, some of these parents made inquiries at the county office, even searched records for farms owned by Finns or worked by Finns. Nothing has come up that fits the profile of your parents, so they say."

I jest sort of nodded.

"They are contesting your eligibility for the contest," continued he, "questioning your true address, requesting an interview with your parents, if, they note, your parents even exist and can be found."

"They can't be found," says I.

"I thought that might be the case. Can you fill me in?"

"My parents are gone. My mom passed from illness when I was young. My dad died a drunk, destitute. I live on my own, out in the forest. I'm trying to make my own way."

Orion nodded and expressed his condolences. He then sort of stared blankly in thought for several moments.

"Did you hear about this Dr. Knotts fella's auction?" asks he.

"Yes," says I.

"His behavior during it was rather bizarre."

"How so?"

"Well, really it started before the auction, right after you all performed your Tom and Becky scenes. I saw him in the theater lobby after the show. He appeared rather distracted, somewhat excited. The next day at the museum, unexpectedly, he suggested he may withhold some auction items, including the featured Huckleberry Finn pipe. Said there'd been a new development, a big one, that would shock the world and prove quite a boon not only to the auction but perhaps the future of the museum."

"Did he say what this development was?" asked I.

"No," said Orion. "He just said he needed a little more time before he could announce it, and therefore was hosting the second auction after the finals of the Tom and Becky contest."

"Mmm," says I, playing dumb.

"Why do you think he'd do that, Mark?" asked Orion. "Wait till after the finals of the Tom and Becky contest?"

"I'm not sure," fibbed I. "He seems like a very strange person."

"Well, that's true. He is strange," says Orion. "Do you have reliable shelter out in the forest?"

"Yes," says I. "Found an old cabin. It suits me fine."

"Found an old cabin, did you?" Orion smiled and his eyes twinkled again. "You can always stay at my house."

"I know. Thank you."

"The parents who are questioning your eligibility for the contest," said Orion, "they are meeting tonight in the museum's great hall, after closing time, to talk about matters with the judges and the Chamber of Commerce and museum folks. I'm going to attend."

"Okay, well, I'd prefer to stay in the competition." I's already thinking about how I might listen in on that meeting.

"I'd like you to stay as well. On a hunch, I filled out some paperwork at the courthouse. It might come in handy. I'll update you after the meeting."

"Okay."

Orion moved toward one of the telescopes and scooped up his tablet. "Let's get back to skygazing," said he.

He highlighted the Mars, Saturn, Jupiter, Moon cluster for me. Then, using his tablet, pointed me toward a small, hard-to-see dot which he said made a possible new candidate for a Goldilocks planet.

But then, the cuckoo bird started singing. Orion's brow wrinkled. "Wait here," said he. "Let me see who this...Do me a favor, keep an eye on that zone with the Goldilocks candidate, okay?"

"Sure," says I.

Not long after he went for the door, a line appeared in my telescope's view. Orion was drawing on his tablet. I watched the cursor closely through the 'scope. He made the letter K, then N and O. He was writing fast. T, T, S. *Dr.*

Knotts! thinks I. Sure enough: KNOTTS HERE, it read, GO. That's all I needed to see. I shimmied down one of the beams holding up Orion's observation deck, scurried across his backyard, hopped the fence, and wove my way toward the museum, a-wondering as I went if I'd be able to stay in the competition, what angle Dr. Knotts was taking by going to Orion's, and what it was Orion had been up to at the courthouse.

CHAPTER SEVENTEEN

I made it to the museum and entered an hour or so before close. I quick-stepped into the great hall and sort of milled about near the raft on which they'd placed Jim and me. When a lull in the flow of people occurred, I went to the ground and quick-slid under the raft and waited.

Seemed powerful long, but in time I heard 'em start closing up. Several minutes later, by peeking out from my spot under the raft, I saw feet walking about. Heard a couple voices. Orion and another fellow was setting up chairs in preparation for the meeting. Soon others straggled in.

"This is a waste of time," I overheard Mr. Testa say. "Who cares where the boy's from or where his parents are?"

"Classic stuff here," said Mrs. Hawkins. "A parents meeting before we've even picked a winner."

About then I overheard greetings directed to Mr. Smullens; shortly later to Mrs. Klein. By and by it sounded like the parents arrived. A Mrs. Carmichael called everyone together, asking the attendees to slide their chairs in and make a circle.

"Hello," said she, addressing the group. "On behalf of the Chamber of Commerce and the Tom and Becky competition, I appreciate you all coming to meet on short notice. These are peculiar circumstances and given the emails being sent about, I thought it best to get you all in the same room to discuss matters. As additional representation for the Chamber, I brought local jeweler and Chamber VP JJ Sloan with me."

Mmm, didn't know he was here, thunk I.

"The issue at hand," continued she, "it seems to me, is that some of you think one of our finalists for Tom should be deemed ineligible for the competition. Is that correct?"

I expected one of the parents to answer. But surprisingly judge Smullens shoveled.

"Yes, that's right," says he. "I've looked at the information Mr. Wallace and Mr. Lewis emailed out. It does appear that there is reason to believe that Mark Finn does not live in the district. His parents don't seem to exist."

"Are you suggesting they never have?" Mr. Testa said, dubiously.

"Listen," interjected Parker-Wallace's pap. "I know I'm Parker's father and he's a finalist and not having

Mark in the competition helps my boy, but the bottom line is, this Mark kid should've never gotten this far in the competition to begin with. No one's heard of him. No one's met his parents or can even show that they exist. He's performed oddly at the various stages of the competition, as well. I mean, gambling? Apparently he ate butter at the formal dinner, as well, and talked about smoking cigars. This competition is a big deal. It means a lot for our town. It can mean a lot for college prospects, for personal development. This contestant, Mark Finn, has no business representing our town as Tom Sawyer, or as anyone else for that matter. He's not from here. He walks around barefoot or in moccasins. His papers are probably bogus. He's not one of us. He should be removed from the competition."

"I agree," added someone else, might've been Charlotte's father, maybe Sterling's—I warn't sure.

"What exactly do you all mean by that?" asked JJ Sloan, throwing in his shovel. "Saying he shouldn't be able to represent our town and he's not one of us?"

"He's not from here," says Parker's father. "He's unkempt. He doesn't wear proper shoes. He seems rather uneducated. He doesn't fit. I mean, have you seen him?"

"Yes, I have," says JJ Sloan. "Now, you do know that Mark Twain described the actual Tom Sawyer as mischievous and disobedient. Tom Sawyer skipped school to go swimming, routinely snuck out of his own home, lied, and played tricks on people, including his own friends. He was also a good friend, courageous, loyal, and many more things. Now let's consider Huckleberry Finn, one of Tom Sawyer's buddies, whom Mark Twain called ignorant and unwashed, and whom he presented as foul-mouthed and uncouth. Of course, he also said Huck had as good a heart as any boy ever. So where do you get off saying Mark Finn, who you don't even know, can't win the Tom Sawyer competition and represent our town when both Tom and Huck were described in a similar fashion to the way you just described Mark?"

"Oh, come on," says Parker's father. "We're more established now. He's probably a runaway anyway, from the 'bottom of Arkansaw,' as he says. Whatever that means."

"The southern portion."

"Yeah, whatever. Do we really need to have someone like that representing our town? We can send him back there. He's not from here. He doesn't qualify. And even if he did, he shouldn't represent us."

"So, we can't have someone standing in for Tom Sawyer who might very well be the closest thing we actually have to Tom Sawyer!?" countered JJ Sloan.

"That's absurd," said Parker's father. "By the way, I haven't even had a chance to talk about another matter. This Randy fellow. Do you know what kids are saying at school? That he seems, shall I say, a little peculiar?"

Mrs. Klein clutched her purse.

"Are you out of your mind?" a lady said. I tried to place the voice. Then it come to me, 'twas Mrs. Brown, the judge who rarely revealed much. Her voice sounded animated now. "These are kids. Give it a rest. You must be kidding me."

"I'm just saying…I heard some kids are saying…"

"Give it a rest," said Mrs. Brown, more sternly.

"Listen," Mrs. Carmichael of the Chamber interjected, "this meeting is about Mark as Tom. Seems to me, we can go around and around forever on the matter. But, really, there's a basic question at hand: does Mark Finn qualify to be considered for Tom Sawyer. Our rules and regulations say you need to be a resident of the district. So we need to find out where the young man actually lives and where his parents or guardians are. It's that simple. Shouldn't be that difficult."

"I have a proposal," interjected Orion. "Let's confront the young man on the matter tomorrow, early afternoon. I'll bring him here, to the museum, to meet with you Mrs. Carmichael, as well as with the other judges. We'll settle the matter once and for all."

"Sounds like a plan," says Mrs. Carmichael.

"And if it's not clear where he lives or who is parents or guardians are, he should be removed from the competition, right?" says Parker's pap.

"Fine," says Mrs. Carmichael.

"And don't think we won't fight this as far as we need to take it," added Parker's pap.

The meeting broke up. I waited under the raft for everyone to push off. Turned out, Orion stayed the latest. When it was jest him left, I wiggled out. Boy, was he surprised to see me.

On the walk to his house, Orion told me that Dr. Knotts had visited his house to ask about me. Apparently he'd heard I knew Orion. He asked Orion of my whereabouts, and told him I was wanted by Family Services in Indiana. He even suggested that he was my rightful guardian. Upon hearing this, I realized that Dr. Knotts was ready to enlist the help of the authorities to profit off tyng me in person to his artifacts. *The gumption*, thunk I.

I considered telling Orion everything, of Dr. Knotts and his crew finding me in the ice while on one of their shady missions, pumping me with chemicals, and planning to turn me into an exhibit; of me escaping and setting up camp in Rolling Dunes, of Family Services and the cops bringing me in, of me breaking free—all of it. But I warn't ready.

Instead, we walked mainly in quiet till Orion says, "As if Dr. Knotts snooping isn't enough, you've got the Wallaces and the Lewises trying to disqualify you."

I threw my hands up and shrugged.

Orion went quiet again before saying, "We should make sure you have a guardian."

"How do you mean?" asks I.

"How about tomorrow we go down to the County Courthouse. You can declare yourself homeless and request that I take temporary guardianship of you, to which I'll agree. That'll buy us ninety days for your case to be reviewed by a judge. I already sent in the preliminary paperwork on the matter, including having reference letters sent in on my behalf, from a few members of the community. Meantime, you'll be good to go for the competition."

"You'd do that?"

"Sure," says Orion, with that twinkle in his eye.

———

Back at Pap's, I found Ned resting on the bearskin, eating a Baby Ruth, reading Louis L'Amour. He wanted a full rundown on the happenings and warn't surprised to hear that Mrs. Hawkins and Mr. Testa were for me staying in the competition, nor that Mrs. Klein and Mr. Smullens warn't. He warn't sure what to make of Mrs. Brown, seein' as she hadn't said much about my situation. But he considered it bullish that she backed Randy. He was delighted to learn Orion had volunteered to serve as my guardian.

Next morning, I met Orion at the courthouse. His background check had come back clean and the agency hadn't been able to locate my parents, which he'd told 'em would be the case. I presented my supposed birth certificate, answered a slew of questions, some accurately, and filled out a bale of paperwork. By the time we left, Orion had gained temporary guardianship of me.

At the museum early that afternoon we met with President Jack, along with Mrs. Carmichael, JJ Sloan, and the judges. The meeting took place in a room next to Jack's office. When Orion and I stepped in, we found the other attendees sitting around a table. Orion addressed the group straight away.

"Hello everyone," said he. "I appreciate you all taking the time to meet and resolve the question of Mark's eligibility for the Tom and Becky contest. I assure you this meeting will be short and will allay any concerns you might have about Mark's inclusion in the contest."

Mrs. Klein let out a heavy sigh, more like a skeptical *ummph*. Mr. Smullens rolled his eyes.

"As you mentioned yesterday, Mrs. Carmichael," continued Orion, turning toward her, "the only real questions are where does Mark live and who are his parents or guardians? Well, both of those questions are easy to answer. First, as this document shows..." he held up the temporary guardianship papers... "I am Mark's guardian."

There was an audible gasp.

"And he lives with me," added Orion.

"Let me see those papers," said Mr. Smullens. Mrs. Klein wanted to see 'em too.

"Sure," said Orion.

He handed them to Mrs. Carmichael. There was quiet as she looked them over and when JJ Sloan did the same. He passed 'em to Mr. Snullens.

"These papers were signed today!" declared Mr. Smullens.

"That's right," says Orion.

"This is ridiculous," says Mrs. Klein.

"You can't just suddenly claim you're his guardian and expect us to let him in the competition," said Mr. Smullens.

"He's already in the competition. And I'm not just claiming to be his guardian. I am his guardian, for the next ninety days, at minimum. So," continued Orion, looking again at Mrs. Carmichael, "you know who his guardian is and where he lives."

"Interesting," said JJ Sloan, with a slight smile.

"I demand a vote," says Mr. Smullens.

"No vote is necessary," says Mrs. Carmichael, eyeing the paperwork again. She looked up. "The judges of the competition don't determine who's eligible for it. The Chamber does. The matter is settled." She looked at me. "Mark, you are more than welcome to stay in the competition, and I wish you luck."

"Thank you," says I.

Mr. Testa and Mrs. Hawkins grinned. Mr. Smullens and Mrs. Klein looked rather perturbed. Mrs. Brown kept her poker face.

———

"Judge Smullens and Klein didn't look pleased," said Orion on our walk to his house after the meeting.

"Not one bit," says I.

"They were asked, I'm sure, to do the bidding of certain parents, who won't be too pleased either," said he with a smile.

"Thank you, Orion," says I.

"No trouble at all, Mark, no trouble at all," said he.

We walked in happy silence a stretch. As we approached Orion's house, he said, "Again, you know you can stay here if you'd like, right?"

"Yes," says I, "but I'm pretty used to staying out in the forest."

"In that old cabin?"

"Yes," says I.

"Don't suppose it has floorboards?"

"It does."

Orion smiled.

"Well, Mr. Finn, you're always welcome here," says he.

I nodded and pushed off. Wound my way to the cabin expecting to find Ned, but he warn't inside. My nerves jumped. I looked for a note alerting me to his whereabouts but didn't see nothing when of a sudden I heard a scooting sound coming from the corner from which we'd dug our tunnel. Moments later, Ned popped his head through and clumb out.

"Just tidying up the tunnel," says he.

We got out some snacks and chewed the fat. Ned mentioned the local newspaper online. "That Dr. Knotts made some flamboyant statements," said he. "I think I've figured out what he aims to do, you know, what's going on and why he's waiting till after the finals of the Tom and Becky competition."

"That so?"

"It's so," says Ned, pausing a few moments. "Finn, I'm not going to press you on all the details. But what I think might be the case is truly incredible. I mean, genuinely out of this world. But no matter how amazing, what matters is you're my friend, and I want to help you."

"Thanks," says I. "It's a bit of a pickle. I can't jest up and leave with Lucy mad at me."

"Yeah."

"I need to see the Tom and Becky contest through, to get on better terms with her, explain things, hopefully help her understand where I'm coming from and where I plan on going in life."

"My guess is Dr. Knotts won't show up at the picnic," says Ned. "It'd be too odd. I think you'll be okay there. But he'll be at the naming of Tom and Becky. And he'll try to make a big show of things in front of the media— and of course bandy his DNA methods to claim proof and quickly look to profit off the news with his second auction."

I nodded. "So the question becomes whether or not I should hi-tail it out of here before the naming of Tom and Becky?"

"Look, you've told me how you feel about Lucy. Win Tom, alongside her winning Becky, and in the process win her heart," declared Ned.

As I nodded, the makings of a way to wiggle out of this pickle ambled to mind. "Let's work out a plan," says I to Ned.

CHAPTER EIGHTEEN

We strategized late; didn't awake till deep into morn. 'Twas too bright and sunny to risk checking my lines, so we jest ate snacks and drank Coca-Cola and fine-tuned our plan. By and by, I dug out the Spacelander and rolled over to Randy's, with whom I'd head to the Tom and Becky picnic.

I found Randy and his sister Sharon and brother Mikey out back playing volleyball, which, they explained, was one of the games we'd be playing at the picnic. They learned me the rules and had me give it a try. It didn't come natural to me. I felt like a tangle of arms and legs, a mashup of mishits and bumbles. Randy laughed and Sharon just shook her head. But they was nice about it and tried to learn me quick.

By and by, the time come to leave for the picnic, which was at the jeweler JJ Sloan's house. His place, I soon found, sets on a cliff above the Mississippi. 'Tis powerful big and made of stone, and features sprawling grounds, a big pond, sweeping views.

Dropping us off, Sharon said, "You need to be on your best behavior. And don't forget, when it comes time for the games, they're going to tell you it's for fun. You need to try to win."

The sun shone bright through a clear blue sky as Randy and I walked up the Sloan's drive. Ahead, we saw a handful of kids playing on a large field of grass. Tucked back aside this field set the large pond, into which a dock stretched. A couple of girls, looked like Lucy and Stacey from afar, was out on the water, standing side by side on what appeared to be long, wide boards.

"Look at this place," says Randy, pulling his sunglasses down over his eyes. "They even have paddle boards."

Another girl out on the pond, looked like Charlotte, was pedaling a small paddle boat made to look like a swan.

"Now this is a picnic," says Randy.

We crossed the front yard and walked along a brick pathway to the main entrance.

JJ Sloan's wife welcomed us in.

We passed by the main living room and entered the kitchen area, which opened to an eating area with floor to ceiling windows that looked out to a large deck boasting wide views of Old Man River. "Hits all the right notes. Beautiful home, Mrs. Sloan, beautiful home. Love the aesthetic," says Randy.

Mrs. Sloan smiled. "Well, thank you, young man."

"I see you've met Randy and Mark," says Mrs. Klein, as she happened to step inside from the deck.

"Yes, delightful," says Mrs. Sloan.

Mrs. Klein tried to hide it but couldn't help an eye roll and a sort of little snoot.

"We're going to head outside and enjoy the grounds," Randy said to Mrs. Sloan.

"Fantastic," says she, walking with us back to the front door. "We do light treatments to the pond, so it's great for swimming. J.J. tells me the games will start in about fifteen or twenty minutes. We'll eat afterward." She motioned to a side room off the main entryway. "If you need to change, you can use the dressing room here."

Randy changed into his suit. I was content wearing my cut-off khakis. On our way out to the lake, we saw Parker-Wallace walking up to the house along with his parents and Sterling. Mrs. Brown was coming up behind 'em.

At the pond's edge we waved to Lucy and Stacey out on paddle boards.

"Let's swim to 'em," says Randy. "You and Lucy have some talking to do."

"Sure do," says I.

We peeled off our shirts, ran a few steps into the water, dove full in, and swum to the girls.

"Hello boys," says Stacey.

"Hello there," says Randy.

Lucy smiled and said hi, but she seemed a little subdued. I could tell she was still sore. An awkward pause followed before Randy said, "Stacey, can you teach me to paddle board?"

"Sure," says she. She slid off her board into the water. "Let's try in shallower water." She swum toward shore, pulling the board along. Randy swum with her.

This left Lucy and me, she sitting on her paddle board, me treading water. We didn't say anything for a few awkward moments.

"You think we can talk?" asks I.

"Sure," says she.

She reached down to help me sort of slide onto the paddle board. Only, as I tried to push myself up to sit across from her, the board wobbled. My weight shifted and the board wobbled further, tipping us over into the lake. I's worried Lucy would pop out of the water upset, but she emerged with a smile on her face, grabbed the board, and said, "Let's try this again."

This time we found our balance.

"Listen," said I, sitting across from her. "I'm sorry I didn't level with you about where I's from, and my parents, and the like."

"Why didn't you?" asked she. "I mean, I guess the whole thing made me realize that I don't know you, like at all."

"It's kind of a complicated situation."

"Where do you live?"

"Out in the forest, in a cabin."

"On your own?"

"Yeah." I didn't mention Ned.

"That's a big deal," said she. "Like, you legitimately live on your own? Run your own schedule, make your own food?"

"Mostly. I catch fish, cook 'em up. Grab snacks at Walmart."

"Is it hard living on your own?"

"I've gotten used to it. It's what I know."

"Does it get lonesome?"

"It can," says I. "That's why I came to town. But it's hard to live on your own and do regular kid things—the govment doesn't take kindly to that kind of thing," says I, smiling. She smiled a little at that too.

She thought for a bit before asking, "Where are your parents?"

"They're dead and gone."

"I'm sorry, Mark."

"My ma died when I was young. My pap died a drunk, destitute. That's why I'm on my own. But the other day Orion agreed to be my guardian. Says I can stay with him if I'd like."

"That's so sweet," says she.

"Powerful big of him."

"Are you going to take him up on it and stay?"

"Maybe so," says I, not ready to tell her about Dr. Knotts. We was silent a few moments.

We looked into each other's eyes. Seemed like she warn't mad at me no more.

"I hope you stay," says she.

My spirits lifted at that. "Thank you."

A loud sound went off, like a bullhorn, pulling our attention from each other to the shore. We saw folks waving those of us on the pond to come in.

"Looks like the games are about to begin," says Lucy.

"Yeah, we should be heading in," says I.

I looked beyond the shoreline, out to the house a-ways off, and saw Mr. Sloan and Mr. Testa standing side by side, on the portion of the deck which looked out to the pond. They were gazing our way. It made me smile. Felt like they were pulling for us.

Back on land, Mrs. Hawkins guided us contestants to the sand volleyball court and huddled us together: "You're going to play a series of games today," said she. "The events are similar to the ones at the Tom Sawyer Days Festival, which, as we all know, culminates tomorrow in the naming of this year's Tom and Becky—and the attendant fireworks." We smiled at that. "As Tom and Becky finalists, tomorrow much of your day will be filled with various duties, meaning you won't get to enjoy the games like other kids. So today's picnic games have become quite a fun annual tradition. Play hard and enjoy."

She looked toward the volleyball net. "Beach volleyball is up first. We've partnered you up. Mark and Jessica, you're going to start things off with a match versus Randy and Charlotte, followed by Parker-Wallace and Lucy versus Sterling and Stacey."

As we broke the huddle, Randy leaned toward me and said, "They're mixing up partners to see how people work together."

Jessica and I walked barefoot across the sand to the other side of the court.

"Jessica," says I. "Jest to warn you, I ain't too good."

"That's okay," says she.

Jessica, turns out, was good. I learned later that she counted as one of the top players at school.

Still, Randy and Charlotte started out the match besting us. Once I figured out how to at least occasionally keep the ball in the air and get it to Jessica, we done better. We split the first two games, so it came down to the third. We was covered with sand by then, on our legs and arms, even our faces. No matter, Jessica and me managed to win game three. To their credit, Randy and Charlotte didn't show hard feelings.

Parker-Wallace and Lucy won their match versus Randy and Charlotte. Made me awful envious seeing Parker-Wallace and Lucy give each other high fives after winning points. Their win set up a finals match between them and us. Randy told me to go out there and put a whooping on Parker-Wallace. Unfortunately, the opposite happened. My fumbling and bumbling volleyball play jest couldn't match up with Parker's power and Lucy's skill. During the second game, Jessica and I did keep things close early on. It was then that Parker's pap, watching the match on the side, started making noise. He'd call out things like "illegal hit," if he thought Jessica or me didn't strike the ball right or shout out "nice shot," on a ball before it landed near the line, so as to sort of get out in front of us calling the ball out. I'd gotten used to this sort of noise from parents when I played football with the Rolling Dunes Lakers. Didn't pay it no mind. But I think it bothered Jessica. Still, she did all she could to keep us in the match. In the end, they smoked us like a hog, two games to zilch. Lucy showed grace in winning. And, I must say, Parker-Wallace didn't rub it in like I thought he might.

The next competition called for us to swim, which I warn't too bad at and which allowed us to rinse the sand off. They set the swimming up so that there was two teams consisting of four people, two boys, two girls. The first swimmer needed to swim to a little floating barge out in the middle of the pond. Upon reaching it, a team-mate waiting there would swim back whence you come, then the next two would do the same. Randy and I got teamed up with Lucy and Stacey. While I fared better in the swimming, I didn't have my stroke down quite like Parker or Sterling, both of whom, Randy said, had been on swim teams. Fortunately, Lucy and Stacey could swim fast as trout, whereas Charlotte and Jessica, good as they were at volleyball, swum slow as perch. Our team won the round.

Following swimming, we sack-raced, you know, where you put one leg in a sack and your partner puts in a leg and you hop together like a drunken frog. I got paired with Charlotte. She was a good sport, but Parker and Jessica won the sack-race.

Next, JJ Sloan and Mr. Testa brung out frogs and a measuring tape. "Frog-jumping!" says Randy. We was all excited about this, me especially, seeing as I'd plenty of experience with it. Now, a key to frog jumping, naturally, is getting behind a frog with bounce. Assessing this in advance is the trick—you gotta get a feel for how a frog carries himself, gauge the length of his hind legs, and develop a gut feel. It's an acquired skill, I'd say.

We stepped over to the carrying cages Mr. Sloan and Mr. Testa had set down. Sterling picked his frog right away, but I observed the frogs a mite first. Didn't take too long to determine which one I wanted. Others picked theirs. The girls named their frogs, names like Sunny and Bounder. Parker called his Babe Ruth. I declared mine Dan'l Webster, to which they all jest sort of looked at me.

"Okay, whoever that is," said Randy, smiling.

Mrs. Hawkins spelled out the particulars. Each frog would get three jumps. Mr. Testa was to measure. My frog jumped last in order.

Now, another key to frog jumping is not holding the frog too tight before setting him down to jump. If you hold him too tight, his nerves rattle, which can affect his leaping. Other thing is to gently prod him with a stick to get him to jump rather than prodding him by hand. Using a stick eases the frog's angst because you don't have to get quite as close to him. This in mind, when my turn come, I set ole Dan'l Webster down nice and slow, then gently prodded him with a stick. And what do you know but he went a flyin' through the air, soaring, like the orator Webster hisself.

"Wow," said Mr. Testa as he unspooled the tape to measure. "Daniel Webster opens a big lead."

Upon seeing Dan'l leap, Lucy and the other girls asked for pointers for their next rounds. I gave 'em a couple of tips. Randy said he wanted coaching, too, and Parker and Sterling joined him, to my surprise. In the end, Mr. Webster didn't need but that one jump to win. This meant Parker and me was tied with two victories apiece going into the final event.

For this final competition, Mrs. Hawkins led us inside the Sloans' home, out to their massive deck with the sweeping view of the Mighty. We sat at a long table, Toms on one side, Beckys on the other. Mr. Sloan and several of the parents and judges stepped out to the deck holding pies topped with whipped cream. It was a pie-eating contest.

They lined the middle of the table with the pies and went back in to grab more which they put on a nearby cart if needed. Seemed like the pie-eating was a surprise to all of us. Not even Randy had known it'd be part of this year's picnic. Mrs. Hawkins explained how it'd go: no using your hands, each of the judges stationed around the table could signal whether a pie was fully eaten or not. Had to wait on a signal to move on to the next pie.

"This is awesome," said Parker.

"Yeah, I ain't ever tried this," said I.

The girls were giggling and shaking their heads and looking at Mrs. Hawkins and the judges like they were missing chimney bricks.

"No utensils?" asked Charlotte.

"None," said Mrs. Hawkins, smiling.

"Girls are competing versus each other, boys versus boys," explained Mrs. Hawkins.

She whistled the contest to start and off we went a-eating. My first pie went down without much trouble—although the judges were pretty stringent on declaring whether a pie had been fully eaten or not. The second pie warn't as easy. Stomach started bulging.

Lucy, somehow, downed two full pies and part of another, giving her the victory on the girls' side. Sterling and Randy tapped out after two-and-a-half pies, which left me and Parker. As we'd started in on that third pie, I heard Parker's Pap putting in his shovel, egging Parker on. Somehow Parker and I ate it full. My belly now popped way out. Eating more didn't seem possible. But I didn't want to lose to Parker. I pulled a fourth pie toward me, as did Parker. And then something funny happened. Before starting in on this fourth pie, we looked at each other out the corner of our eyes and, without speaking, said the same thing to each other: *I can't eat any more pie and neither can you and this competition is ruther absurd.*

An even more peculiar thing happened next. Jest as I grabbed the edge of my pie and pulled it upward, sort of toward me but a little toward Parker, he done the same toward me. We smiled wryly at that, paused a moment, and then, looking at our respective pies, had the same thought: *we should chuck these pies at each other.* And at that instant *Smash!* We sent our pies into each other's faces.

"What are you doing!?" hollered Parker's pap.

We were having fun. We smiled through the cream and, without saying a word, grabbed for another pie and went for Randy and Sterling. They warn't expecting it. We got 'em good. In turn, they quick-grabbed pies off the cart and came for Parker and me, only we'd popped up and now was a-running, pell-mell.

"To the pond!" hollered Parker.

"To the pond!" echoed I.

We ran across that deck laughing, out to the yard, bound for the pond, while Randy and Sterling chased us with their pies. I looked back to see how close they was and caught a glimpse of Lucy in the background, the other girls, too, all giggling. And I saw JJ Sloan and Mr. Testa rubbing their bellies, laughing. Right then, Randy's pie come flying through the air and it caught me. Sterling's got Parker. We all kept a-running to the pond, whip cream a-streaming off our cheeks. The four of us hit the dock, sprinted down it, and leapt in the water.

CHAPTER NINETEEN

That evening, Sharon picked up Randy and me from the picnic. I asked if she could drop me at Orion's, and she obliged. I found Orion tinkering away, ready for a break. He grabbed a pitcher of lemonade in the kitchen and poured a couple cups.

"Big day tomorrow," says he.

"Yeah," says I.

"Who do you think gets named Becky?"

"Lucy Thoreau," says I without hesitating.

He smiled at that. "And Tom?"

"Not sure on that one. I guess Parker-Wallace, most like."

"Probably don't need to remind you that tomorrow, after the naming of Tom and Becky, Dr. Knotts is streaming the second part of his auction from the B&B."

I nodded.

He looked at me. "He's up to something," said Orion. "I expect him to show during the announcement of the Tom and Becky winners, looking to stir up noise."

I nodded. "Don't worry," says I. "I've got a plan."

Orion headed to the living room and waved for me to follow. "I've got a couple of things for you."

He led me to his secretary desk, which he opened and grabbed something from. It was wrapped in a little towel. He unfolded the towel to reveal the contents. 'Twas a gold and silver piece, both of which I recognized, as well as a couple of fish hooks. All of it was mine. I'd had 'em when Dr. Knotts and his men found me and thawed me out.

"I won these at Dr. Knott's first auction, anonymously," Orion said. He handed them to me, adding, "But they aren't mine."

'Twas such a nice gesture by Orion. I didn't know exactly how he'd guessed at who I was, but in a way it didn't surprise me. If anybody could figure it out, it'd like be him. As I received the items, I nodded and said thank you.

"I'll be at the naming of Tom and Becky tomorrow," Orion said as we walked to the front door. "If we don't get a chance to talk afterward, I just want you to know, it's been a real pleasure. And, as I've said before, if you ever need a place to stay, consider this home."

"You've been a kind and guiding light to me." says I. "Thank you, Orion."

———

I found Ned in Pap's cabin, sitting on the horse-blanket, looking at his laptop.

"Hey there, Mark, how'd it go?"

"Good. Picnic games was fun, and I made some progress in patching things up with Lucy, I think."

"Did you win the games?"

"Well, I won a couple of 'em."

"Who won overall?" asks Ned.

"Thing is, it sort of—for the boys—ended in a food fight and no clear winner."

"A food fight?"

"Parker and me chucked pies at each other and then at Randy and Sterling. And then them two come for us, and we all ran to the pond and jumped in. It was grand."

"Wow," says Ned. "Did not expect that."

"Parker's all right."

"Okay then," says Ned.

"What're you up to?" asks I.

"I snuck into town earlier, to charge my laptop at a coffee shop. And now I'm reading a message chain amongst the judges of the Tom and Becky contest," says Ned, nonchalantly, like it warn't no big deal.

"What!?" asks I. "How are you doing that?"

"Wasn't that hard to hack into actually. And don't worry, they can't trace it. I have a VPN through satellite internet and a tool that delivers the data in encrypted packets."

I shook my head, ruther amazed.

"Look at this," says he, turning his laptop toward me. He clicked on a link to the "Judge's Portal." A side screen popped open into which he typed weird-looking characters along with the occasional letter or word. He said it was code. Looked like computer sorcery to me. Next you know, he's in the portal, and we can see a chain of messages. The first ones he scrolled through were pretty boring, you know, jest the judges stating when they planned to meet the following day and what their schedules looked like.

But then a message from Mrs. Klein read: The pies in the face today was another example of just how peculiar this year's competition has been on the boy's side. I hope you all take into account that Mark Finn, of dubious background, has gambled, talked of smoking cigars, thrown a pie in a contestant's face, and, oddly, eaten butter off a saucer by the spoonful. I don't understand why he has not been banished from the competition.

Mr. Smullens: I understand your concerns, Virginia. He is a very peculiar figure, and in light of him lying about his background and the other dubious shenanigans, I concur.

Mr. Testa: My goodness, give it a rest. The young man essentially was homeless and without parents. Fortunately, Orion stepped up on his behalf. So he wasn't born with a silver spoon? So he isn't a standard candidate? He is the most interesting candidate I've ever come across in this competition, and the most attuned to the actual times and persona of Tom Sawyer. He should definitely be considered.

Mrs. Hawkins: Listen, you all, we've been through this. It was decided to keep him in the competition.

Mrs. Klein: That was before the pie in the face shenanigans.

Mrs. Hawkins: Well, all the boys were involved in that, and it was pretty darn funny, you've got to admit. The contestants seemed to bond over it.

Mrs. Klein: It's beneath the dignity of the office.

Mr. Testa: Need I remind you that Tom Sawyer played hooky, cussed like a sailor, lied, bamboozled, among other things? Of course, despite all that, as I've said, he possessed a good heart. He cared about his friends, was adventurous and optimistic, imaginative and daring. I think Mark, too, is a lot more than what you're giving him credit for.

Mrs. Hawkins: As I say, we've been through this. He's in the competition. We'll vote tomorrow. See you all then.

"It sounds like you've got a real shot," says Ned. "Mrs. Brown didn't weigh in. But Mr. Testa is a fan and Mrs. Hawkins might very well be voting for you. Of course, Mrs. Klein won't; neither will Mr. Smullens. It may come down to Mrs. Brown."

Next, Ned pulled up a satellite map of St. Petersburg. I pointed out to him where the festival would be the following day and the location of the outdoor stage upon which they would be naming Tom and Becky. He pulled up the description of the festival, including the different sorts of rides and games and food booths it featured. Then we went back over the plan. Satisfied and near wore out, we pulled a few fish off the lines and came back to the cabin, started a fire, and dug out some snacks. 'Fore long our bellies were full and we was stretched out, me on my bearskin, Ned on the horse blanket, regaling each other with stories as we fell out.

CHAPTER TWENTY

We awoke well after the sun. Time was a little tight. I pulled on my cut-off khakis, buttoned up the JC Penney shirt Sharon had picked out for my Tom Sawyer look, and dug out the straw-like fedora hat and suspenders. Ned put on nondescript attire. He planned on strolling the festival grounds, blending in, while I sat through a ceremonial brunch featuring the eight finalists.

We packed the Mother Lode with my bearskin, some snacks and soda, fish line, hooks, matches, and the like. Then I run the Mother Lode to the small canoe I'd stowed, hugging the shore, abreast a little bend, aside a snarl of riverbank bushes.

Ned and I talked matters through a final time before I pushed off. I dug out the Spacelander and wheeled over to the B&B Theater's banquet room. Along the way, I passed downtown's great lawn, near the river. It functioned as the heart of the Tom Sawyer Days Festival. A stage was set up on one edge, upon which we'd stand later that day for the announcement of Tom and Becky. Kids was out on the lawn playing games like the ones us finalists had done at the picnic: sack-racing, pie-eating, frog jumping.

As I approached the theater for the brunch, Parker-Wallace and his family was strolling up. His parents barely looked at me. But Parker flashed a smile. He let his parents step ahead of him a little, then he made a motion with his hand as if he was throwing a pie in my face. I smiled back at him and did the same.

Now, what do you know but I'd plumb forgot my moccasins? No joke. Luckily, Mr. Testa was walking into the theater at the same time as me and when the lady at the reception desk declined to let me in on account of being shoeless, he kindly stepped in and said I was a contestant and fully committed to the costume. She rolled her eyes and reluctantly let me through.

The banquet room was quite spacious, with a high, rounded ceiling. Seating had been arranged on the left and right of a wide center aisle. Place was darn near full, too, with most folks dressed in their Sundays. An usher led Parker and me down the center aisle, to a makeshift stage, at the middle of which was a speaking dais. Then the usher motioned us to a table left of the dais, where Randy and Sterling already sat. Parker and I grabbed a seat. Across from us on the stage, sat the Beckys: Lucy,

Stacey, Charlotte, and Jessica. Like us, they was in costume. Lucy looked as beautiful as ever.

By and by a historian stepped to the dais. He welcomed everyone and had us Toms and Beckys stand up for applause, and then he started in on the lives of Tom Sawyer and Becky Thatcher themselves, what things were like back then in St. Petersburg, and how people went about their business, as well as where things like Grant's drug store and the tanyard actually used to be. He got most of it half right. He talked up the Twain fellow pretty tall, but that ain't new.

After the historian, a member from the Chamber, the museum president, and Mr. Smullens spoke. Judge Smullens talked up the competition and confirmed that this year's winners would get to go on a trip to China, where they'd tour one of the shoe factories his family had partnered with. Finally, the waiters come out with food.

Following the meal, we were ushered outside to a pavilion, to mingle with supporters of the contest. By and by they walked us over to the Tom and Huck Museum. Out on the streets the festival crowd had really grown. People milled about all over the place, and vendors lined the streets, hawking elephant ears, cotton candy, straw hats, and more. People stopped to look at us in our costumes.

Near the museum, kids was lined up for a chance to paint the fence Tom gulled them boys into painting. Out on the great lawn near the river even more kids than before was taking part in lawn games. Us Toms all looked at each other and nodded toward 'em. That's where we wanted to be. Instead, we soon found ourselves shaking more hands, this time in the museum, where we then listened to another dignitary ramble a bit. Once he finished, they included us on a tour of the museum for special guests of the festival, which is short for people with money. At the big display of Jim and me on the raft, I found my chance to come up alongside Lucy.

"Seems so peaceful," says she, looking at Jim and me on the raft, "just floating the river, not a care in the world."

We had some cares, thought I.

"Two friends floating," added she.

"Speaking of friends," says I. "I know you're sore at me for not coming clean about where I live and who my parents are but..."

"It's all right," says she. "I understand better since we talked."

"It's just that, this isn't easy for me," stammered I.

"What's not easy?" asks Lucy, turning toward me.

"Mmm...well, all this, the competition, the..."

"You know, Mark, we may be Tom and Becky," said Lucy, flashing that smile.

"That's the thing. I wanted to talk to you about that," said I, taking a look around. Folks was milling about, chatting. I leaned in toward Lucy and lowered my voice.

"I know you want me to level with you," says I. "It's a little hard to explain but with me not having parents and the govment wanting me, at least the Indiana govment."

"Indiana?"

"I spent a spell there before coming here."

"Okay. Why are they after you?"

"Well, it's kind of a long story, but basically Family Services plopped me in a home for boys without parents. I snuck out."

"I see," says she.

"And there's also this Dr. Knotts fellow."

"The one who ran the auction?" asked she.

"Yes," says I.

"My dad said he seemed sort of creepy," said she.

"Basically, for economic reasons he wants to claim me as his own."

"Really?"

"What I'm saying is I might have to light out."

"Light out?"

"You know, get…" I started to explain further when of a sudden Mrs. Hawkins interjected.

"Hello you two," says she, glass of wine in hand. "You both look fantastic. Have you been enjoying yourselves?"

"Oh yes," says Lucy. I nodded as well.

"Well, good," said Mrs. Hawkins. "You two make a cute pair." We blushed.

As she pushed off, I turned back to Lucy only to hear her pap say, "Oh, there you are."

He walked toward us. Clearly this warn't a good place to talk in private. I looked at Lucy and said on the quick, in a near-whisper, "Can we talk later, a few minutes to four?"

"Sure." She looked baffled.

"At Lover's Leap."

"Lover's Leap?"

"Yes, there's more I want to say."

She nodded jest as her Pap reached us.

As I stepped away her pap said, "Good luck, Mark."

"Thank you, sir."

Randy walked up alongside me.

"How'd that go?"

"Pretty good, I guess. It's hard to talk with all these people around."

"You two are going to win, and you'll have plenty of time to talk."

"You don't know that. You might be fitting to win."

"You two are Tom and Becky. I've got a feeling."

———

Finally, the time arrived to put the fedora on this year's Tom and the bonnet on this year's Becky. Chamber officials and a couple of museum reps walked us to the festival's main lawn near the river. Now the lawn was filled with even more people, as was the festival booths surrounding the lawn. People again eyed us as we passed by in our costumes. As we stepped up to the stage, a whole lotta folks turned their attention to the ceremony.

Naturally, the back-patting and introductions and all the pomp commenced again. It was during this that I saw the suit-clad henchman with goggles who, all them weeks back, had talked to me on that bus bound for St. Louis. He nonchalantly had taken up a position out front of center stage. When our eyes met, he nodded to his left, then to his right. Men dressed jest like him was watching the stage, too, one of 'em looking calm as a housecat, his leg up on a hay bale, as he puffed a cigar; the other, tall and broad, stone-faced looking more serious. Didn't surprise me none to see 'em there. I glanced back at the goggled henchman. He was looking right at me and this time when our eyes met, he nodded toward the back of the crowd. My breath caught when I looked thataway and saw two policemen. *Mmm,* thinks I, *Dr. Knotts has decided to enlist the help of the authorities.* I guess he thinks they'll help him bring me in and from that point, he can figure things out. Either way, if I get outed, his auction and other plans get more attention.

I was distracted, but in the back of my mind I heard Mrs. Carmichael say, "Without further ado, it is time to announce the winners of this year's contest. First, Becky. Again, we want to thank Charlotte, Jessica, Lucy, and Stacey for all their hard work and passion in this process. This year's Becky Thatcher is Lucy Thoreau!"

The crowd cheered. Lucy hugged the other girls and then stepped up to the dais. Mr. Sloan placed a bonnet on her head to signify the honor.

"Now to Tom," Mrs. Carmichael said, smiling. "We want to thank Mark, Randy, Parker, and Sterling for their hard work and passion during this process as well. That said, this year's Tom Sawyer is Mark Finn!"

Hearing my name surprised me. Cheers rose up from the crowd, and I was guided to the dais, where Mr. J.J. Sloan replaced my fedora with the official Tom Sawyer one. "Congratulations, Mark," said he, shaking my hand.

I looked at Lucy, and we embraced. "Can you believe it?" said she into my ear.

"No," said I, scanning the crowd over her shoulder.

Dr. Knotts's goggled man was standing near the front of the stage now, whispering in the ear of Jack, museum president. A policeman stood next to him.

"We would love for you two to share some words," said Mrs. Carmichael. "Becky, you first."

"I can't thank the judges and the chamber and everyone else involved with this contest enough. To my fellow contestants, it's been a joy going through this process with you. Any of you all would've made a fine representative of our town. I'm flattered to be named Becky Thatcher and am excited to serve in this role alongside Mark Finn as Tom. Thank you again."

"Mark, a few words," says Mrs. Carmichael.

As I stepped to the mic, I passed by Lucy and whispered, "Don't forget. Lover's Leap, jest before four." She nodded.

I looked out over the crowd. I'd never spoke to this many folks before. "By jings," says I. "This is something. I've got to hand it to the judges, my fellow Toms, and all the folks involved with this competition. They gave me a fair shake even though I'm a ruther uncommon sort and a little uncouth and unlearned and low down. But I do think I have a feel for ole Tom Sawyer, and I appreciate the judges recognizing that. I dare say I could trick Tom's own Aunt Polly into thinking me's him." I looked at the judges. "So for you to grant me the honor of being Tom, no matter how foolish and whaling and disobedient he was, I'm quite grateful. Tom had a big heart, was a dear friend, and his adventurous spirit and imagination made him a true original." I paused a few moments. "All that being said, I think it's important to recognize a couple things right now. First, Lucy Thoreau is going to make a great Becky. To be named Tom to her Becky is truly something. However, she deserves a great Tom and the truth is, somewhat unexpectedly, I gotta light outta here. I'm new here to you all and yet you've welcomed me. I'd like to stay, but that can't happen right now." I turned to Randy. He looked confused. The crowd did, too. "Randy, can you step up here." He did so. "Luckily," continued I, "my good friend Ned read the by-laws to this competition. And they say that if the winner can't carry out his duties as Tom, he can pick one of the other finalists to do so for him. So, with a tip of the cap to Lucy, I'd like to present to you this year's real Tom Sawyer: my good friend Randy."

At that, I slid the Tom hat off my head and put it on Randy's. He looked at me flabbergasted. Then I turned, quick-stepped to the side of the stage, and jumped onto the lawn. One of Dr. Knotts's men started for me. I side-hopped past him and took off a-running through the crowd.

I thought I was in the clear when of a sudden a man stepped out from behind a tree trunk and tripped me with his cane. 'Twas Dr. Knotts. I tumbled to the ground hard and whacked my head on the ground.

A little dazed, I stood up and felt Dr. Knotts grab me by the arm. I managed to spin and yank away. Off to my right, jest off the street, was a funhouse of all things. I ran to it, hopped passed the ticket-taker, and snuck inside as Dr. Knotts hollered, "That's my boy, I'm going in."

CHAPTER TWENTY-ONE

I turned a corner and found myself in a large room of mirrors, spaced in a kind of half circle, staggered at different depths and angles. I zigged one way, then the other. I went deeper into the room. No matter which way I went, the mirrors made it look like there was thirty of me, well, it made it appear as if there were thirty Tom Sawyers seeing as I was dressed like him. Between all the mirrors and being a little dazed from my fall, I couldn't tell exactly how to get out of the funhouse. I heard a noise, turned around, and froze. It was Dr. Knotts. He had his cane pointed outward, like a sword.

"Listen, Mark," said he. "We can do this the easy way or we can keep doing this the hard way."

I stayed quiet, didn't move a muscle.

"Come in, boy. Come home. That's all. Come to daddy. I will make you more money than you'll know what to do with. Together, we can tell the story of the ages, provide hope for the great elixir, change the world as we know it. Just come in. Come to me."

Now I noticed something while he was talking to me. His eyes sort of danced, as if they were bouncing from one mirror to the next. It dawned on me that he didn't know which Tom Sawyer was Huckleberry Finn.

My head begun to clear. I still had a chance to get out. I needed to get a feel for which Tom he thought I was. So I made a sort of appeasing face and gently held my hand out, as if to say, "Okay." He stepped toward me. Well, he stepped toward what he thought was me. He had a mirror in mind. I waited for him to take one more step. He did. And then *Boom!* I crouched low and lunged forward for a tackle and wrapped up his legs, jest like Coach Rogy taught. He hadn't expected the angle from which I struck. It took all I had, but it was enough to make him go down. And when he went down, I popped up and took off a-running, for the exit opposite the way I came in.

Popping out of the funhouse I was vaguely aware of a commotion at the ticket-taking booth. I slid under a rail and jumped off a little walkway into the street. Ran pell-mell, weaving here and there through the crowd, without looking back. I figured some of Dr. Knotts's men had seen me and would be a-coming, maybe the cops, too. After a long stretch going full-tilt, I glanced behind me. Sure enough, a couple of Knotts's men and a copper were trailing.

About a quarter-mile on, I'd gotten through much of the crowd. I looked back again. My pursuers were still a-coming, but I had a good lead. I turned onto Mark Twain Avenue for a stretch. Felt like I'd outrun 'em when a cop car with lights a-blazing turned onto Twain Avenue jest behind me. The car screeched to a halt. Glancing behind me, I saw two coppers jump out. I angled off toward the cemetery, weaving a bit through it, before popping into the forest. I had maybe fifty yards on the coppers, but they was fresh.

Yet I know the St. Petersburg forests, and I used that to my advantage, bouncing off a trail here, picking up another there. Several minutes later I was only a few hundred yards from Pap's cabin. I could hear the coppers behind me, though. I jumped a fallen tree branch, landed, and went to churning again. Finally, I made it to Pap's, pushed open the door, and rushed inside. Ned and I slammed the door shut and each of us placed a log across a notch. Ned turned to me.

"They're right behind me," said I, catching my breath.

He nodded and hustled me to the tunnel. "Time for a magic trick," says he quietly.

"Permeation," says I.

I slid down into the tunnel we'd dug and reached up to shake Ned's hand. I heard a loud voice call out, "The cabin, he's in the cabin."

Ned and I looked at each other. "Thank you," says I, keeping my voice low.

"Forget about it," whispers he. A knock at the cabin door sounded. "When they figure out who I actually am, they'll send me home and my mom will be happy. Get going."

As I slid through the tunnel, I heard Ned holler hysterically, "No, don't come in! Wait. I need to talk to someone." He was buying me time.

I eased out the tunnel into the middle of the snaggle of junipers. Ned was still carrying on, loud and kind of incoherently. Slipping from tree to tree in the thick forest and stepping lightly but quickly, I covered ground. Soon I made it to the river's edge and the canoe I'd stowed, which I eased out onto the water. I slid into the canoe and lied low as it floated downriver. I used a long stick to reach over and guide me time to time, but mainly I stayed low in the canoe. If you didn't know better, you'd've simply figured an empty old canoe had gotten loose.

I rolled downriver jest past downtown before sitting up and guiding the canoe toward a forested stretch of bank. There I clumb out, with the Mother Lode, which I'd stashed within, and, staying mostly hid by forest, made for Lover's Leap. My legs burned as I climbed uphill through forest. There were a few, long switchbacks before I come out to a rocky stretch which angled its way to Lover's Leap. When I got out in the clear on that rocky stretch, I saw that Lucy was up ahead. Seeing her warmed my heart, put more horse in my step.

Upon reaching Lover's Leap, I must've looked plumb wore out.

"Mark, are you all right?" asked Lucy.

"Yes," says I, trying to breathe regular. "Appreciate you meeting me here."

"Yes, of course. I mean, it is kind of romantic. Our first meeting as Tom and Becky at Lover's Leap…except that you're not Tom anymore. Randy is," said Lucy, looking at me. "What's going on?"

I swung over the little guard fence and helped her do the same. We stood at the edge of the cliff.

"I can tell you this…" started I.

"No, you need to tell me everything. Seriously."

I did not want to lose her.

"You're not going to believe me," said I.

"Try me."

"Okay. I'm Huckleberry Finn."

"What!?"

"I said you wouldn't believe me."

She stared at me. "Please explain."

"As you know, at the end of the *Adventures of Huckleberry Finn*, I lit out West, to Apache country. Well, it was too hot there. Have you ever been to Arizona or Nevada in the summer?"

"No."

"It's incredibly hot. Incredibly hot. Ridiculously…"

"Okay, I get it. And…"

"I signed up for an Arctic adventure, to be an explorer to the nether regions of the Arctic Ocean. It sounded bully; seemed like the only thing that could cool me down. Anyway, we got shipwrecked, hit an iceberg, and I was near death on an ice shelf when I decided there was nothing to lose by trying to traverse the sheet of ice we'd hit. Doing so, I fell in an ice hole. Global warming melted me out jest in time for Dr. Knotts to find me, pump me full of chemicals, and bring me back to life."

"Dr. Knotts?"

"Yes. That's how he got his Huckleberry Finn artifacts. He wants to turn me into a kind of global exhibition, study me, stick me with needles, parade me about, and in the process make a boatload of money."

"What do you want?"

"I want my freedom. I want to build a life on my own terms. They won't ever let me alone if I let 'em take me in. It'll be like I'm a zoo exhibit. I gotta get lost."

Lucy thought for several moments, trying to digest what I was saying.

"Hardest thing," says I, "is that I like you, Lucy. You're kind and smart. You're funny. You read. You're beautiful. You got sand."

I took her by the hand.

"I see how most kids," continued I, "have a mom and a dad and sometimes it makes me kind of sad, you know, seeing as I lost my ma when I was just a little boy and never did really have a dad. But when I'm with you, I see a future, a future that one day includes me being a good dad, living a family life, on our own terms, free and happy, out in space, maybe in a place like Montana."

Lucy smiled.

"I know it probably sounds crazy."

She looked me in the eyes. They were tearing up. "I like you, too," said she.

We leaned towards each other and kissed. I think the sun paused.

We pulled away when the town clock chimed its first of four bells. A freighter, right on time, blew its horn to let St. Petersburg know it was rolling through. I looked to my right and what do you know but coming up the gradual incline of rock on some sort of mountain-four-wheeler were Dr. Knotts and a couple of his henchmen. *They are relentless*, thinks I. I turned back to Lucy.

"I know it's a lot to take in, and we're young. But I'm never going to meet anyone like you. And I don't want to lose you. I just gotta go for a while. But I'm gonna write to you."

"How? From where?"

"Believe me, my buddy Ned'll help me get in touch with you in some encrypted sort of way or somesuch. And, later, I'm going to come back for you, if you'll have me."

Tears streamed down Lucy's cheeks.

"Don't cry," says I. "What we have is a beautiful thing. We just have to keep it alive."

I looked down over the steep edge of the cliff. The train was getting closer. So was Dr. Knotts. Lucy and I hugged.

"Enough of this, time to come in," said Dr. Knotts, having made it to the guardrail.

I glanced quickly over the edge of the cliff, then turned to Dr. Knotts and his men before looking back at Lucy.

"I love you," says I. Then I turned around, eyed the train one last time, and jumped off the cliff.

When free falling some twenty-five feet through the air, worry creeps in: *did I time it right? Am I going to die here?* I turned to my side a little to brace for the impact. Then *Boom!* I hit a hay bale hard. Wind rushed out of me, but the fall didn't knock me out. I kind of bounced off the first big hay bale I landed on and come back down onto the next bale. I held on something fierce. *By golly, it worked,* thunk I. I was alive on top of a hay bale, getting carried west by a freighter. I turned, sat up, and looked up toward the cliffs. Looking down at me was Lucy Thoreau. Dr. Knotts and his henchmen were gazing down at me, too. But they warn't really in the picture. I only saw Lucy.

I smiled at her and waved.

She waved back as I drifted west.

I cherished the thought of us meeting again.